CAUGHT IN A LIE

EMILY TALLMAN

Caught in a Lie. Copyright © 2019 Emily Tallman. Produced and printed by Stillwater River Publications. All rights reserved. Written and produced in the United States of America. This book may not be reproduced or sold in any form without the expressed, written permission of the authors and publisher.

Visit our website at www.StillwaterPress.com for more information.

First Stillwater River Publications Edition

ISBN-10: 1-950-33944-0
ISBN-13: 978-1-950-33944-0

1 2 3 4 5 6 7 8 9 10

Written by Emily Tallman.
Cover design by Kat McConnell.
Published by Stillwater River Publications, Pawtucket RI, USA.

*The views and opinions expressed in this book are solely those of the author
and do not necessarily reflect the views and opinions of the publisher.*

"Hypothetically. I mean… If you have a case… It's for my paper. Anyway, if you have a patient, a compulsive liar, how do you get them on a better path without ruining their life?

"How do you, as their trusted confidant, tell them to start being honest when you know that everything will blow up in their face? Do you keep the old lies and start fresh or do you take the addiction route and admit the problem and apologize or… or is there something else?"

"Well to start with, what exactly do you mean by compulsive liar? You know the studies aren't exactly trusted source material and depending who you talk to compulsive, pathological, narcissistic, and sociopathic could all be considered the same. Liars."

"I'm talking about simple definitions here. Where Compulsives lie habitually to avoid the discomfort of social anxiety or as a way to prove to others that they're worth talking to. Story tellers. Exaggerators. Not manipulative, but consciously lying to improve their lives or at least make themselves sound better. Not Pathological as in lying in response to stimuli or continuing to lie even to those who know they're lying. Or lying about things that make them sound worse just for attention."

"Are you sure you're not being manipulated by a really good liar?"

"Positive."

"And this is all hypothetical of course…"

"Yeah. For the paper."

"Well, they've got to tell people the truth. Your job is to better their way of life. Anyone who can't understand or only wants to stick around for the lie is not bettering the patient's life."

"Telling the truth." Jaeli breathes out, emptying her lungs and feeling suffocated at the thought. "All of it?"

"I don't see any other option." Alex folds her hands over one knee and leans forward in a classic therapist move that's always been so natural for her, "Do you want to talk about it Jae?"

"I guess I have to."

CHAPTER ONE

"Guess what happened at work today!" Catherine's falsely cheerful tone rings through the phone. *Great, it's going to be one of those nights.*

"Oh, I don't know. Kira was a narcissistic bitch, the smelly guy was smelly and… they fired more people and the replacements are drooling dolts? Jaeli leans back and pokes at her cereal, it's going to get soggy. There's no way around it. A call with Catherine, not Cathy, nicknames are tacky is never just a quick call. One needs to be prepared for at least a half hour of whining, another fifteen minutes of begging advice, yet another half hour of listening to why that advice wouldn't work and then a good ten of her picking apart *your* life. And dear lord help you if she heard chewing or heaven forbid, a TV. Cereal wasn't really a great dinner choice anyway. Maybe if Jaeli orders pizza she could beg off when the delivery man rings the bell? It hadn't worked the last five times, but there is always hope. Or at least the insanity of repeated actions offering the same results.

CAUGHT IN A LIE

"Mom's right, you're psychic. And no… I always pictured people you would call 'dolt' might have some kind of redeeming adorableness about them. Like a stupid little bunny rabbit. But seriously now, guess what happened!"

"I don't know Catherine, tell me." Jeali rolls her eyes and scoops up some milk just to watch it splash back down when she tips the spoon. It's likely going to be the most exciting thing to happen tonight.

"Well, Kira," *here we go*, Jaeli thinks, it's always Kira, "got flowers every hour on the hour today! Can you believe that? Her boyfriend must be rolling in it. Any way the first one got there at nine and she wasn't even in yet, typical."

"Don't you guys get there at eight thirty?" Jaeli asks, playing along. It's a set-up, she kind of had to.

"I *know*. She's infuriating. Anyway, they got there and they were red and ya know, like a dozen but then every hour was a different color and the bouquets just got bigger and bigger and they all had cute little notes with them and the last one even had a teddy bear. It was adorable. Why do the assholes of the world get the nicest boyfriends? *And she's even cheating on him*. It's ridiculous. If I had a man like him—" Yeah she is definitely ordering that pizza. Jaeli pulls out her laptop and worries at the mouse pad impatiently while it boots up. "But what about you, any campus cuties to crush on."

"God no, they're all babies. They're either twenty two years old or the 'slightly older students' aka: fifty year old divorcees."

"Twenty two's not bad."

She's going to roll her eyes straight out of her head tonight. Twenty two isn't bad for Jaeli maybe, but Catherine's fifty point list for the perfect man would never include someone with their own set of student loans. No, they'd be older and refined. Maybe have had a full ride to Harvard or at least their daddy's wallet paving the way for them. Maybe she's being a hypocrite thinking it but… "No just broke with a BA and big eyes for the future but no actual job lined up. I can't coach people through emotional and economic crisis at work and at home, Catherine. I need to come home to an emotionally and financially stable someone."

"Don't you think you're being a little picky?" Probably, but Catherine doesn't need to know that. Jaeli is just fine by herself. If picky means she has a somewhat valid excuse to be single then, so be it.

"Says the two dates and done queen." Jaeli says in a teasing tone to her big sister, thanking her lucky stars when the doorbell rings. "Um, sorry Catherine, I need to get the door. Might be my study group already—"

"You didn't say anything about—"

"Yeah, Sorry. Bye." She hangs up, looking at her phone all the way to the door almost in shock when her sister doesn't ring right back. "Huh."

Jaeli pays for the glorious smelling pie and over tips by a distracted accident but she doesn't really care once she takes the first bite and it is cheesy heaven. Screw freshman fifteen, carbs are beautiful and she will never think bad thoughts about them again. Besides, she isn't a freshman anymore. Grad school is different. All the take out calories she would ingest will be almost immediately dissolved away by the crazy stress and forgotten meals of extra work and running across campus. It'll be fine.

Three bites in and her phone is ringing again. MARIANNA, the screen glows at her. Crap. If Catherine is a piece of work, Marianna is the rest of the pile. She puts down the heavenly slice and closes the box, her older sister's problems have a way of stealing her appetite along with her patience.

"Hey Mare."

Jaeli sits through a few minutes of awkwardly listening to her big sister cry before she finally opens up. "I don't know what to do anymore Jae. He just won't listen. I've shown him the bills, the bank statements. I've emptied my 401k. He's not even fazed. I don't

CAUGHT IN A LIE

think he ever actually filed for unemployment like he said. And *why?* How can someone be so lazy and watch the bills come in and just accept a piece of shit fast food job when we have nothing left? How are we going to pay Scott's tuition? He's got to get out of this Jae, I can't make Scott quit college, he's got to get a good job and get out of here. And Ariel. She wants to be a doctor. *Why is he doing this!"*

"I know Mare. But like I said, maybe you should think about—"

"I'm not leaving him. Not yet. Not until the kids are out." Marianna says coldly.

"You won't even think about it?"

"I can't."

Jaeli sighs. She knows why she is in school for her masters. Knows why she is going into psychology as her field. It's not that she has always wanted to be a therapist, it's that she's pretty sure she's been one since she could talk. Her first word, told by her mother again and again to everyone like Jaeli was the most adorable, curious kitten the world has ever seen, was 'why?'. But Jaeli knows she wasn't asking how something worked or what something was. She remembers asking why her mom was crying. Why Marianna was mad and why Catherine was so scared. She gets it now, almost, how a man can twist up your life and the way you think. Dig himself in and control everything and leave you helpless. "Why?" Maybe Grad school will show her why Catherine craves that fate so badly or why Marianna won't take her daughter and get out of there or give her family a way to help them.

Her sister starts crying again and Jaeli sits back in her chair sniffing back some tears of her own and trying to stay calm. Getting organized isn't happening tonight, but she can't bring herself to care when she is pretty sure hanging up on this call would lead down a very dark path for her family.

It's eleven twenty-seven and like clockwork her phone rings again. Every night, after eleven twenty-five but before eleven thirty her mom calls to wish her good night.

"Hello my darling. How was your day?"

"Fine mom. Nothing exciting."

"No, no. It was your first day. Tell me who you met, what the professors are like, how exciting are the classes. Come on open up to me Jaejae." She sighs and pulls the pizza box towards her. Ma would understand if she mumbles around her food a little. She has probably just gotten off the phone too. "Are you crunching? Why do you eat so late Jaejae? That's not good for the stomach or your mind. You will have strange dreams and get thighs like me. Nobody likes thighs Jae."

Jaeli rolls her eyes and sets down the slice for the second time. She can't help the agitated tone that comes out, she's frustrated at the day and might be just the tiniest bit hangry. "Yes ma, I haven't had time to eat yet and I won't be going to bed for a while so I think its fine."

"No need to shout. Now tell me about the day."

"It was fine." Jaeli pretends she doesn't hear mother's disapproving hum. "Went to class, got assignments, got pizza, talked to Catherine and Marianna and now I'm trying to eat the pizza."

"And the night, tell me of that too."

"Slept fine. It's probably the best night's sleep I'll get all week. I have a lot of reading due already ma, I can't talk long."

"Tell me about your dreams darling. Let me tell you what they mean."

"Ma, I don't have—"

"*Jae*" She snaps back. This is her mother's way of telling her that she is having a bad day, maybe even that she's worried or lonely. If Marianna had given her the same emotional speil as Jaeli had just gone through, her mother probably just needs someone to tell her something nice. So Jaeli does.

"Snow." She lies, she can't really remember her dreams unless they're the special ones.

"That means news darling."

"I know mom." Jaeli closes her eyes against an incoming headache and sees a face against her eyelids. Oh right, him. "Had a dream about a man. Handsome, rich, very sweet. Okay?"

"Hmm. I like him but what happened to the girl?" The girl had been another lie. An image her mind conjured up and something her mother has latched onto for whatever reason.

"I told you ma, I think we'll be friends." *Yeah right.* Her dreams have never really meant what her mother has wanted them to, the special ones, reoccurring ones or otherwise. She isn't going to meet the mystery girl or guy. They are probably just people she's caught a glimpse of on campus, just brain trash.

"Oh, so you think the boy is more? I hear you roll your eyes at me. You do not dream of people you have never seen, Jae. Not unless they are important and you will see them soon. Yes?"

"I don't think so Mom. In my dream he's in trouble. Something to do with a broken window."

"That is bad. Windows hold reflection or maybe a path and his is broken. He doesn't know who he is or where he's going. Trouble, yes. Maybe I don't like him so much anymore." Her mother's accent tilts up in what Jaeli has heard when her mother is trying to joke, but this time she senses the nervousness in it. Old women and their superstitions.

"Alright, enough about mine, I don't really remember what happens anyway." Just the words bring a splatter of blood across a creamy colored carpet to mind. "So. Tell me yours."

"Babies."

"Mom, no one is—"

"No, no, no, a very dirty, sick baby that I cannot help. It is filthy and heavy and I put it down to get help but then I cannot find her and every time I do another piece is missing. It's so bad Jae and I keep putting her down."

"Hey, hey. You're not a bad mom, ok. We're grown up and we've made our own choices, good or bad and we have to live with them. Ok? You can try to protect us from things in life but you can't protect us from *life* mom. Marianna is going to figure it out and she and Ariel will get out of that house. I won't let Jason hurt them. I just need to get Marianna to admit that she needs help. And Catherine has dug her own hole, moved in and built an impenetrable wall around it. None of this is your fault. Alright? And I'm ok too, I'm stressed but I'm fine."

"You are so smart my little one. I don't have to tell you anything. You have the gift."

"Yeah, and next I'll make tables float like great grandma back in Sardinia, I know. Hey, when it happens maybe I can make the big bucks, huh? Fix everyone's problems?"

"You don't need to help *everyone* Jaejae, just help *you* and I will die happy. You get married, make money and babies and show me you are ok and I rest happy."

"Don't say stuff like that ma."

"It is truth. Now go dream. It is not good to stay up so late. Do your reading tomorrow. Maybe write about the dream and make the teacher happy with how you know meanings. People like that you know."

Jaeli smiles at the phone as she hears her mom kiss it and hang up. Maybe she's right. Her work would probably come out better with a little sleep anyway. It's only the first week, she can't let herself get too stressed already, family matters aside.

CHAPTER TWO

Jaeli Tal has always been a bit of a dreamer, but no amount of dreaming is going to get this paper done on time. "I did not sign up for this crap" she mumbles to herself as she taps away at the keyboard. Only, she kind of did.

Creative writing. As a grad student, it's a requirement that she take a writing course. Expository was her first choice but that was taken over quickly by journalism, English and history majors. And no way was she going to torture herself with Creative Writing – Poetry. So Creative Writing – Fiction it was. Now, it's Sunday night. That means she has had six days of stressful calls, multiple mind melting psych lectures and chapters to read with no essays written. And two are due in the morning.

The first, the more important in her mind as it pertains to her major, is a journal entry detailing her most traumatic experience. They would be handed in, checked off by the teacher and then passed out anonymously en masse amongst the class to be analyzed as an intro to the course and to each other, without the pressure of knowing each other's secrets. It's an odd assignment, but Jaeli couldn't pretend she's not interested in knowing the deepest, darkest secrets of the people around her. Four assignments like this are on the syllabus and she was fearing them, until this moment. Two AM the very morning the assignment is due is not the time to dwell on her own deep, dark feelings.

On top of that is the absolutely ridiculous Creative Writing assignment. One she would have to read in front of the class and would be in no way anonymous. She had thought it would be easy, juvenile even. Basically a show and tell.

Show and tell. Ridiculous. Completely.

And terrifying.

Because like her Psych class it has to deal with personal experience, though this time it has to encompass both ends of the spectrum. In example, starting incredibly happy or sad and moving to the opposite emotion. Angst with a happy ending or a bad decision shattering your perfect day, and it has to be based on at least one real experience. Jaeli is kind of actually lacking the bravery to write anything about herself down on paper.

She just doesn't think she's that interesting. It's why she had gotten in so much trouble for fibbing when she was younger. That could be her excuse right? She is twenty-five, she hasn't had any life changing moments yet, not really anyway. Nothing touching either end of the spectrum, everything just kind of floating happily or sadly in the middle. Sure, she's had fun, but nothing indescribable or hopefully anywhere near the happiest moment of her life. And the same with trauma. She's had some hard times, but things could always get worse and she doesn't want to cheapen anyone else's experience with her silly little, abandonment issues or insecurities. Insecurities are for burying, hiding, sometimes even from yourself. And right now, at two in the morning, she's having trouble digging them up.

Jaeli sighs and leans back to stretch, thinking on her life so far. She has her Bachelors in Psychology, which didn't really take her anywhere in her field outside of internships and office jobs. She had wanted to take a year off, get some experience in her field, save up a little money, maybe make a small dent in her student loans but one year turned into three when she had gotten stuck in a comfy job. It wasn't anything spectacular, just a clinician's office, eleven dollars an hour with health benefits. It was nice, but it wasn't what she wanted. She wants to help people, not schedule appointments and input counselor's notes. She wants to be the one taking notes, and as nice as free dental is in this day and age, she decided that she had to go back to school.

Now she's here, enrolled, studying, and terrified. Was this the right move? She's only twenty-five but she feels old on the college campus and like she doesn't really fit here anymore. Honestly, she never really did, but what few friends she had have moved since college – settled down, started jobs or Masters programs right away.

She got stuck behind.

This is supposed to be a fresh start, a blank slate. But there's no such thing as a blank slate, is there? You can apply to a new school in a new city with new people, but you're still you. Under every blank slate's shiny surface is matte paint and the grains of wood or whatever else cheap ass material goes into the things. The point is – there is a past there, under the shine, and the same goes for Jaeli no matter how many times she tries to change her look and herself and pretend otherwise. As a psych major, she should really try to analyze that part of her personality. What makes her depend so heavily on the camouflage or costume of fibbing? Maybe it goes back to her need to please or the constant, crippling fear of failure. According to her latest text book, it is undoubtedly her parents' fault.

She looks at the Creative Writing online syllabus again, *Assignment One* is highlighted with the little blurb the professor added in after talking to the class.

Go home and write about the best or worst experience in your life and turn it on its head. Good to bad – Bad to good. Be ready to share and receive criticism and evaluation from your peers next time as an introduction to the class.

And remember: Writing is easy. All you do is sit down and open a vein. – Emily Dickenson

Opening a vein is just about what Jaeli wants to do right now.

This is one hell of a personal introduction. And who the hell is she supposed to introduce? She's nothing. Nobody. Sure, there's been death and depression, ocd, and the occasional dabbling into the eating disorder category when she was younger, but nothing ptsd worthy, right? At least nothing she hasn't repressed the hell out of. And no, probably nothing to begin with. Hard times aside, she's led a pretty privileged life.

And then the Psych paper! What were people going to analyze about her? The clock ticks over to two thirty, a half hour wasted on fretting and only seven hours left until she has to leave for her ten AM Creative Writing class with Professor Jacobs and straight on to her one PM psych with Dr. Sommers. No time to finish a paper between classes if her first didn't let out early, and how could it with sharing and criticism? Even if it did, that only leaves her an hour. If she can't get it done in seven, she definitely can't get it done in one. She needs to *focus*!

The only thing standing out to her is her father leaving when she was three, but that didn't really have an effect on her emotionally at the time. She can barely remember it, barely remember him. Of course it affected how she grew up, but she wouldn't call it a traumatizing experience. That would be more for her mother and sisters.

Jaeli's fists clench closed and her eyes open wide. Thinking of her mother gives her an idea. A really stupid idea, a two thirty AM with no sleep and a class in seven hours idea.

Dreams need analysis too, darling.

This is such a bad idea. This is technically lying. She could be honest and open about it, could say she has reoccurring dreams with vivid detail that affect her emotionally for her psych paper…and maybe leave that out of the writing one? It is creative writing after all. Fiction, no less. Why are they writing truth?

She has a sour feeling in her stomach, she can't do this. She's a good student. A front row dwelling, graduated with a 3.85 GPA, only brought down from that stupid advanced biology gen ed she should never have signed up for. Why write about a silly dream when she could actually talk about her experience with depression, make some like-minded friends and allies, get some potentially helpful feedback? And issues, she has big issues, obviously, if she's contemplating this.

But does she really?

How many of her classmates are going to take this assignment seriously? It's just one assignment, and this is just one class. The first real class after introductions. There's plenty of room for improvement from here on out. Realistically, she is probably not the only one up writing a horrible paper right now. And if no one else is taking it seriously, why should Jaeli stress herself out about it?

Dreams really do need analysis, more than life sometimes. They are where you hide your deepest fears, and secrets, and those pesky insecurities. And, well it is her own brain trash so… why not?

The clock in the corner of her computer screen turns over to two forty four and her decision is made. She opens a new document, makes two cover sheets and closes her eyes, just for a second to concentrate on the dream and begin writing. The man's pained face appears behind her eyelids with stunning clarity and it hurts to see him like that. Suddenly it's so easy. She finds herself writing a romance novel and something she is struggling to keep in character for herself. She writes hopes and maybe private, subconscious dreams and fantasies of being rescued that she hoped were still believable and wouldn't show her as a weak, overly feminine sap but rather a strong, in charge of her own life lady that maybe was once a bit young and naive and got a little swept away in a handsome face and heavy wallet.

Come on, what's a little maladaptive daydreaming to escape her own drooling day to day life between classmates? It's just creative writing. She could be creative.

The story starts like everything else in her life, with a phone call.

CHAPTER THREE

*I*t was a phone call then too, just a few weeks from her third birthday. Jaeli barely remembers Marianna treating her like a doll. Putting bright eyeshadow up to her eyebrows and tying a scarf in her teased-up baby hair. They were giggling and playing dress up, Marianna and Catherine talking about what their father would be bringing home from Texas. There was always something. Clutter, their mother called it, but the three girls were fascinated with the renaissance fair knickknacks. Little homemade goods that looked like they came from another time or far off land or were stolen from the fairies. Jaeli would get to see them first hand when she was a little older and her father would weasel his way back into their lives over a summer vacation or two, but tonight she is blissfully unaware of such magical items. She plays with sticky glitter lip gloss stuck between her fingers and listens to her sisters' babble back and forth. They hear the phone ring and Marianna and Catherine bolt from the room yelling a mix of Daddys! And Let me talk to him! When is he coming home?

Jaeli stumbles to her feet in the too big skirt her sister has tied around her waist and toddles after them. Their mother has a funny look on her face. One Jaeli has never seen. She's speaking the funny words too but Jaeli isn't laughing at the nonsense like usual. And then the yelling starts and Catherine picks her up and takes her back to the bedroom. Her face is red like before when they were playing in the snow. Jaeli reaches out to touch it and smears glitter on her sister's cheek. "Stop it!" Catherine yells, slapping Jaeli's chubby hand away. She hears her mother shriek down the hall and the noise scares tears to her eyes. She's confused and scared and starts to cry. "Shut up, just shut up! You don't even understand! This is all your fault! He didn't even want you! You were a mistake!"

***

"Everything happens so fast, and I realized that there can't ever be a happy ending because that's not the real end of the story. All stories end in tragedy because eventually everybody dies even if they were loved. And isn't that like falling too? I heard him say he loved me five times today, he never heard those words from me. I had the perfect relationship with the man I loved. I loved him and he didn't have to love me back, but when he did it tipped the scales. I felt so good that something had to come take it away and put balance back into the world." Jaeli clears her throat and shuffles her papers back into order. That…was not easy. It felt much bigger than a fib, making someone up just to kill them off.

She doesn't know why she thought it would be, but speaking in front of so many people was rough, especially with everyone on edge from their own stories. If she felt so bad here, she didn't know how she was going to handle listening to people analyze it. This is bad. She looks back up at the girl she has unintentionally been reading her story to the whole time. She is a tiny blonde girl with a blue streak in her hair and a few too many piercings for Jaeli, but they suited this young woman nicely. There's something familiar about her and it's a bit more comfortable to just pretend it was the two of them instead of 20 other bored faces and a squinting, judgmental professor. "So, that's it. The end."

Jaeli goes to move back to her seat, but Professor Jacobs puts up a hand, one finger pointing up more proudly than the others, and stalls her as he flips back through his own copy of her story. "Comments class. Then you can sit down Miss Tal."

"Sad, man. It was interesting throughout. I was wondering when it was going to turn bad." A heavily bearded guy in the back speaks up first. Ok, that wasn't so bad.

Another man goes next, this one a little young and looking like maybe he spent the night partying over writing the paper. His flannel shirt is wrinkled and covered in stained streaks and there are dark circles under his eyes. She almost feels bad for him. "That was really harsh for like, a young person to go through. It almost seems kind of like a fairy tale. Like, I'm not saying it would never happen, but it's a little cliché. The rich foreign prince falls for the insecure college girl."

"I never said he was a prince." Jaeli says with a smile and a shrug, the criticism stings a little even if she deserves it. It was just a dream. One she had filled in a lot of blanks on. She shouldn't feel so invested, but she isn't used to doing a poor job, especially in front of so many people. Did she mention she hates this assignment?

"No speaking until the end Miss Tal. Anyone else?" That grated on Jaeli's nerves, how is she supposed to take criticism if she can't ask for a backing on the feelings? She straightens her shoulders and waits for the next blow.

"I know it was supposed to be bitter sweet, but I guess I just don't see the sweet. It looked like he wasn't such a big deal and the end was the emotional part. Maybe you could have showed us more of the friendship before this bad day?" Jaeli bites her lip and nods at the woman. She looks to the next person and the next, each having a comment that eats away at her patience. This class is going to blow. She obviously doesn't have the creativity or experience for creative writing. And just thinking that is churning her stomach. The thought that her psych class is going to see this same paper in a couple hours… they'll know it's fake. If it can't pass for a silly short story, it won't pass for fact. What was she thinking?

"I thought it was really powerful. The end was somehow still a surprise even though I knew it was going to take a bad turn. Good job." The girl with the piercings says. At least someone likes it.

"Was it a good job Alexandra?" The professor asks, standing and gesturing Jaeli back to her seat. "I think the consensus is that the ending doesn't fit the story. That it came as a shock. That shouldn't happen with the written word, not like this. Especially with everyone knowing the assignment. I think Miss Tal's story could have done with a little more foreshadowing. Or any foreshadowing really. At least you have something you can improve upon for your midterm editing assignment. Comments or questions from the writer?"

Jaeli suddenly feels like she is about to have the material for the perfect answer to this assignment. Her brain clicks on as soon as she hears the words leaving her mouth, but it's too late. Here she is, saying words that will not only impact her grade but the rest of her life, she can feel it.

"There is no foreshadowing in real life. I'm not psychic."

Jaeli freezes at about the same time that Professor Jacobs does. He blinks at her behind his artsy glasses before adjusting them and stuttering out a "Well, then. My apologies, but the comment stands. When editing go back and put in details you might not have noticed until after. Something for the audience to notice even if your characters do not. Next. Alexandra?"

Nice going Jaeli, she thinks to herself, *maybe some caffeine before class next time, hmm?*

***

CAUGHT IN A LIE

Leaving class after that disaster is easy. Getting down the hall—not so much. As soon as she is through the door, she feels a hand on her shoulder. "Honey, are you okay? That must have been so hard."

"Uh... not really? I mean, I knew what I was getting into. I just got a little sensitive, that's all."

"Still, that was very brave. You did a great job. I don't think I could have written about something so close to home." The woman, Trisha she thinks, keeps saying as Jaeli tries to walk down the hall. She is tall and thin with beautiful dark skin and big trusting eyes. Crap. This is her chance to say it wasn't real, no big deal. She made a mistake, being honest could fix it. But then Alexandra is there and the frat bro who is apparently named Dan and they are all heading to psych with her. *Fantastic.* Trisha squeezes her shoulder as they pass through the next door and find seats.

"Thanks." Jaeli says, her cheeks flushed red in embarrassment. She is never going to survive this. *Three* people in her class are going to know which paper is hers. She's almost thankful for her little dramatic lie to Professor Jacobs, it would avoid at least three people thinking she was lazy. How did her screwed up brain ever think this was okay? Grad student or no, she is never writing a 3am paper again!

For what has to have been the most stressful two hours of her life, the class wasn't that bad. There is no reading aloud, just papers passed in and sent off with a TA so everyone in class could have a copy. Better than her creative writing class where she had to kill a forest with her own dime so everyone could have a copy to read from.

They discuss a chapter on some theories that would be studied over the semester and their first year, and schedule supervised clinician hours that will be happening at the campus offices. They won't be able to practice, supervised or otherwise, off campus until they're eligible for their licensing exam. There were pros and cons of taking a break before getting her masters. Before, she would have had to study two years to get her masters, work 2000 clinician hours while studying two more years to get her Certificate of Advanced Graduate Study. Now everything has been streamlined into one, three year program which she is going to work her butt off to hopefully cut into two years, two and a half if her ambitions fall a bit short.

Somewhere in her busy schedule she is also going to have to work in monthly or more appointments with her own clinician as part of the program to develop connections in the world of psychiatry and experience examples of how to lead a session. All in all the next year, at least in this class, doesn't sound so bad.

It seems their stories aren't going to be as big a part of the semester as she had originally thought. Looks like they are going to be read now, commented on this week and then again with their more educated opinions at the end of the semester. At the end of next semester, they might be used as a bonus on the final.

That is another thing she hadn't been expecting, apparently she's stuck with this group for two semesters. Trisha approaches her desk after class lets out and asks Jaeli to lunch. Maybe that isn't such a bad thing.

As the semester goes on she gets closer to Trisha and Alexandra, she may even call them real friends and eventually the lie is forgotten. Well, at least until little things come up that make the three of them remember. When it happens, there is always an awkward moment to follow, a forced segue or two, and then everything goes back to normal. Jaeli doesn't know how to tell them the truth and thinks it's for the best that she just doesn't.

It would have been one thing to tell them right away, but months later is a serious breach of trust that she's ashamed to have committed. She lets herself make up for it by being a better friend in other ways and moves on, hoping they will too.

Her therapist doesn't agree with this line of thinking of course. Jaeli is encouraged to tell the truth on a bi-weekly basis but she just doesn't want to risk it. Eventually, Jaeli lies to her therapist and tells the woman what she wants to hear to get her off her case. She's a bit worried about what will show up in the notes and if her professor will have access to them, but as the semester goes on everything is kept confidential. The only time sessions are even brought up is when diagnosis from different student are passed around to write their final papers on. It's extra credit if you can connect a diagnosis from the list to an essay from the start of class.

The list haunts her a little, making her wonder which things are being written about her and who connected what with her paper. *Compulsive liar* stands out amongst the rest. Is that what she is? Was that one hers? Did just one big lie give her that title? Or was it the continuation of that lie? No, it has to belong to someone else.

Jaeli's in the computer lab printing out her final essays for each class and looking them over, remembering semesters past when she was convinced her final essays were always the worst things she would ever write and proving herself wrong with the next year's assignments. She's just waiting on the dreaded creative writing assignment to be spit out of the over worked, under inked nexus when her phone rings.

MARIANNA flashes on the screen. God, now what?

"Hey Mare, can it wait just a few hours? I'm just finishing up on campus and then I'll be on my way home. Promise."

"I need to borrow some money Jae."

"Mari, I can't you know that. Have you tried mom or Catheter?" She brings up their dictionary definition middle sister's old nickname in hopes of lightening the mood. If the wet chuckle on the other end of the line was any indication, it works.

"You remember why we called her that right? I can't ask her. And you, you're back at school if you can afford to do that you can help us out right?"

EMILY TALLMAN

Jaeli's heart breaks a little. She can't, just because her student loans were put on furlough when she went back to get her Masters doesn't mean she's rolling in it. The opposite actually. She took out the maximum amounts they would give her so she could scrape by with an internship for credits and a part time job in the campus store. When she gets out, she is going to need to be hired immediately, if not sooner, and she'll still be looking at a life of debt. Hopefully it will be worth it. That being said, between textbooks, a laptop she didn't have to rent and her apartment, she doesn't have much to spare. But family is family. "How much are you thinking?"

"Ten?"

"Please tell me you mean dollars?"

"Thousand?"

"Marianna! How are you that far set back? Who do you owe that much to so quickly? Sorry, I'm not judging, but gods!"

"It's just everything. Jason's car broke down again, mine needs work if he's going to take it on the highway every day for work, Ariel's school is having a trip, then there's the mortgage and heat, water, electricity, cable. The holidays are coming up—"

"Mari, hold on. I'm trying to listen okay, but do you need *all* of those things? Just listen!" I snap, knowing my sister is about to jump down my throat. I'm already getting evil eyes from the furiously typing procrastinators without the volume from the other end of the line amping up. "I know, heat, home, electricity, water, ok. But maybe cable can go away for a little while? And Jason's car isn't even inspected, is it? Maybe sell his and yours and get *one* car that actually runs for over a month at a time? And don't think about the holidays yet, we'll figure that out. Now, stop panicking and think of what needs to be fixed right away. How much do you need?"

"That doesn't change anything."

"And wait, why does Jason need to take the highway to work, not that I condone your death trap car, but I thought he got a job at Saltys?"

21

CAUGHT IN A LIE

"The one in New Haven."

"*Connecticut*? But isn't there like one in every town now? I can think of three in West Warwick alone. Why is he driving over an hour away for part-time work at minimum wage?"

"Because that's what he does. He's comfortable in take out and it's what was hiring."

"There's take out everywhere, MickyD's and coffee shacks are always hiring. He can't use that excuse."

"Name a chain he hasn't been fired from under ugly circumstances, Jae."

"Well if that's true and if you're really going to lose the house, then maybe it's time to leave that comfort zone."

"Spoken like a true therapist."

"Not yet."

"Yeah, well you should try telling him. He won't hear it from me anymore. He won't hear that we need more money in the bank yesterday. We need—"

"You *want*. But your funds aren't supporting the lifestyle you want right now. Ok? It doesn't have to be this hard. We didn't have cable growing up. Do you really *need* that right now?"

"Television is the only escape I get. Literally the only thing I enjoy right now."

"Well you have the internet don't you? For Ariel's school work?"

"Yes." The tone isn't one Jaeli would say is a good thing, but she's going to keep trudging through with hopeful thoughts of a nice quiet lunch and a long, peaceful car ride home for the holidays. If she could just finish up here and calm her sister down before Catherine and her mom start calling about the same issue and how they should fix it. She knows Marianna, and this isn't going to be a one call thing, but if she could at least get her to think everything over, maybe tomorrow's call would be better.

"Then can't you watch your shows on the computer?"

EMILY TALLMAN

"So my TV is a useless hunk of overpriced junk?"

"For now, or maybe you could sell it? Just for now Mari. Then you could save a little money and make a little money. Maybe? How much would cutting out the cable bill save?

"I'd still need at least ten thousand."

Jaeli is losing her patience. It's a ridiculous number that almost has her worried that Jason was stupid enough to see a loan shark, but deep down she knows Jason has to have some kind of love for his family even if he is a lazy asshole about showing it. He wouldn't put them in danger like that, would he? He's done some risky stuff before, but karma was always quick to bite him in the ass. She thought he had learned his lesson by now. "Well, I don't have that kind of money. Not even close. I'm sorry."

The line goes dead and Jaeli can only assume that Marianna's hung up. She doesn't have time to be worried right now. She puts her papers together and gets out of all of the rushing students' way. She tries not to think about it as she goes to each professor's mailbox to drop off her work and attends her last psych class of the semester. She tries not to think about it as she finishes packing up and putting any perishable food she still had in her fridge into plastic bags to take home with her. She locks up her little apartment and skips lunch, not thinking about it all the way back to Providence. Then she sucks it up, calls her sister back and lets her cry and complain. She could handle just being an ear. She'll leave the advice up to their mom.

CHAPTER FOUR

"*I do too! Just because he couldn't make it to Winter Ball this year doesn't mean he doesn't exist! You guys are so immature." Jaeli says, trying to remain calm.*

"Yeah, and I'm sure he lives in Canada too." Jamie says, heavy on the sarcasm.

It's not fair. They've been taunting her all day. 'Sweet sixteen and never been kissed.' They'd been chanting it, driving her nuts. No happy birthday, no balloons on her locker, no little presents at lunch, just teasing. It had always been teasing. Since elementary school, nothing but bullies and idiots. She had to make it stop somehow. "No. I just really only get to see him in the summer when the fair is in. He travels the whole country for work and when I'm old enough I'm leaving you jerks and this stupid state and going with him."

"Sure. And you're his summer lovin' and in New York there's Abby and in New Jersey there's Jen—" Sarah starts.

EMILY TALLMAN

"Don't forget Tina from Texas!" Megan is happy to throw in.

They're laughing again and it makes her so mad. Why was it so hard to believe that someone would love her? "He doesn't have the time for a girlfriend in every state. He works. And when he's done for the day he calls me and when we're not talking he writes me the most beautiful love letters. He's a man, unlike the little boys you date. He loves me."

"Oh! A man!" Megan laughs, braces shining.

"Yes, a man. He's thirty. He knows how mature I am. Unlike you." Their eyes go wide, Jamie's eyebrows almost disappearing into her hair. This time it's Chelsea to speak.

"Thirty? Seriously? Ew. What a creep."

The teacher reminds them all that some are still taking quizzes and Jaeli lets it go. Thirty was probably a bit much, but that's the age all the hottest movie stars are so she didn't see what the big deal was. At least not until the next Monday when Mrs. Flynn calls her to stay after class and explains how even if we love people, sometimes they don't have our best interests at heart. They can be selfish, and Jaeli should really consider telling her mother about this man. Of course. They never believe a word out of her mouth, but now she's being abused by an imaginary boyfriend.

***

Jaeli gets home on December 21st this year, incidentally the first day of winter which is always an affair in her mother's house. There's baking and decorating and of course picking the best log money can buy or ax can chop to carry all of their hopes and dreams into the fire with it and burn through Christmas and into the New Year. Jaeli never really got the tradition. As an angsty teenager, she used to think it was about managing expectations. Burning your hopes and dreams and all that. As an adult, she is sure the tradition goes back to picking the biggest and best logs to heat the home or camp through winter and make the holidays more comfortable. Her current holiday is not comfortable.

Coming home for the holidays is never quite like the Christmas songs. Sure, there's snow on the ground and sparkly consumerism left and right, but the bickering and extra per diem work hours don't exactly put magic in the air. That and working the front desk of a clinician's office during "the most joyful time of the year" isn't all sugar plums and candy canes. It's almost enough to test someone's motivation towards their dreams. But this is still what Jaeli wants to do, maybe even more than going home. At least at work she can help people. Home... home is chaos. Very opinionated chaos.

Most opinions currently flying around are regarding what Marianna should do about her money situation. Jaeli is trying to stay out of it the best she can. It really isn't any of her business and her opinions aren't popular according to the family census. But it looks like, for the twelve days of Yule and Christmas, her sister, Jason and the kids are going to be staying at her mom's house with Jaeli.

"What is that?" Jaeli asks, stepping back from a curious ball of matted fur, sticks, and various other detritus.

"A cat, what does it look like?" Jason asks, dropping a heavy box down with a thump too close for the cat's comfort, it seems, as it jumps and hisses. Jason has that effect. Jaeli watches as the matted ball of dirty fur sneaks out the back door when Marianna opens it to come in with her bags.

"I thought all pets except work animals were unnatural?" Jaeli addresses her sister ignoring her idiot brother in-law. She's not trying to be rude, but when you hear nonstop complaints about someone like Jason for months it's hard to have a good opinion of them.

EMILY TALLMAN

"Well," her sister sighs, giving her husband a glare Jaelie tries to ignore. "Jason and Ariel think I'm stupid and old fashioned. So meet Mud."

"Mud, huh?"

"Well that's what Ari insists she was covered in when we found her. I personally have never smelled mud that foul. Either way, it's what she keeps tracking all over the house."

"Fun."

"Yeah. You're telling me."

"Mm. You tell mom we have another guest yet?"

She'll mostly stay outside. What mom doesn't know won't piss her off."

"Fun." Jaeli says again, not at all looking forward to the fight she's sure that line of thinking will brew up.

You would think the daily phone calls would stop now that she's only a few minutes away from both of her sisters, but no. And being home with her mother is nice, she has missed her fiercely, but it's a lot of pressure when she's grown used to a stressful routine and lonely little apartment. Sure, between being overloaded with classes, an internship, and part time job, there isn't much time to herself. All work and no play makes Jaeli a dull girl and all that. She won't worry about it until she's repeating that line all the time. When she had finally put her phone on silent and snuggled in for the night, all she needed to worry about were her idiot neighbors having a loud party. Now, she has people just walking right into her old room to borrow things, ask questions, or worst of all, just sit next to her and watch her register for classes or order books. It's something that never used to bother her, the intimacy they all shared. Maybe she needs to be socialized again like the poor cat hiding in her closet. She'll try her best on Christmas.

Soon enough the day is there. As Secret Santa presents are passed around, Jaeli watches Ariel open hers. Her niece is easy to please. Anything involving one of her favorite TV shows would do really, but Jaeli went a little overboard price wise with tickets to Rhode Island Comic Con. Or at least promises to buy them as soon as they were available written on a post-it attached to a lanyard with her famous crush's face plastered all over it. She had hoped it would just make the girl smile and not feel so stressed out by her parents bickering on Christmas. At least she got the smile. She's sure her nephew isn't helping, currently making fun of the DVDs she knew Ariel had saved up to buy him, complaining that they weren't Bluray. Ever since he had rolled out of the frat van a few days after Jaeli arrived home, Scott has been acting the typical stuck up, know it all, college freshman. Jaeli really hopes that he isn't starting to take after Jason.

Jason gets a hooded button up coat. At least he seems to like it, her mother had asked her for help many nights before bed regarding a perfect present for her son in-law. Something he would appreciate and maybe cheer him up a bit. Jaeli thought he needed a good fire under his ass more than cheering up, but she wasn't home so she didn't really know. Sometimes Mari could exaggerate things. Her mother is cooing at him, blowing up his ego to get him to try it on. The coat is nice, but strangely familiar. When he finally puts it on it fits him well, her mother must be proud at how good it looks on him. It must have been expensive. Jason flips the hood over his eyes so all Jaeli can see is his stubbled smile and her gut drops, nerves jolt through her and she has no idea why. He's not so handsome anymore.

"You ok?" Catherine asks, showing off her new bracelet by waving her hand in Jaeli's face, she's glad for the distraction.

"Yeah. Fine. Almost don't recognize him." She gestures at their brother in-law, bald head back out from under the hood.

"Thank the gods for that." Catherine says under her breath. Jaeli struggles to hold in a chuckle.

With antipasto and bread they have a canceled Netflix account and how that is apparently the end of the world when staying at your grandmother's house for free. Jason of course eggs things on with snide little comments and Marianna looks more and more guilty by the minute. Then, for the next course there's complaining about work, how hard it is and how underappreciated they are, but mostly the people they work with. Things seem to be calming down until it comes up that Scott's internship pays more than Jason's new position at Salty's and even Catherine's job of eight years. What revelations the season brings. And to put the whipped cream on the dessert of the feast is criticize Jaeli hour, complete with moving the gingerbread cookies to the other side of the table with a remark about her figure. She checks her phone almost hoping for a work emergency even though she knows the office is closed today. All she gets are some holiday emojis from Alexandra and Trisha. She responds, ignoring Catherine's dating advice, and that's when it happens again.

"Who are you texting? We're still eating."

"Oh, it must be the boy from her dreams. Yes?" Her mother guesses.

There's a moment where Jaeli is half frustrated and half distracted by the dancing reindeer on her phone, she's feeling a bit sarcastic and her mouth speaks without her brain's permission. "It is. His name's Oliver and he says Merry Christmas. So you can quit the harping. And no, he doesn't have any brothers. Just an older sister if you want to give that a try, Catherine." She smiles up at her sister and texts back a dancing Satan gif followed by fire emoji, Christmas tree, fire. The matching shocked faces she receives in response are priceless.

"Oh look, he's making her smile. I like this boy. Why isn't he here? Did you invite him?"

Jaeli realizes that they took her joke seriously and has a moment of panic at doing it again before she takes in their happy, hopeful faces. Even Jason looks interested, probably wishing for another guy at the table. Even when Scott is home from school, the man is seriously outnumbered.

Jaeli's sure there are other options available. She can correct them, can laugh it all off even and leave them wondering. She'll blame the eggnog as she goes on to recite the good pieces of the essay she'd written earlier in the year, lacing in a few tiny facts like Oliver's big sister Rose she'd had to make up for her friends during those awkward little occasions when they were reminded of her fake tragedy and she needed to say something. She leaves out the break in and death scene, just thinking about her still recurring nightmares churning the Christmas feast in her belly, and she says that he's home for the holidays. He is rich after all. He can afford to do things like fly across the pond a few times a year for visits, right?

"So when did you two start dating?" Catherine cuts her off, pushing crumbs around her plate in a manner that doesn't seem at all pleased.

"We're just friends." Jaeli say quickly. It's probably alright to have an imaginary friend, but putting her dream man, her supposedly dead dream man, into a relationship with her is too much for her family to believe. That, and she doesn't have time to maintain the lie. And, you know, it's wrong. She has to keep reminding herself of that. This is all wrong. The essay, the continued little bits she'd throw to her friends and now lying to her family? She has picked a very bumpy road to travel down.

"Why?" Ariel asks, her eyes bugging out of her head like it is the stupidest thing she's ever heard her auntie say. If she only knew.

"What do you mean Ari? We're just friends."

"Yeah, but he sounds pretty awesome. He sounds like the friggin Doctor."

"Language Ariel!" Marianna snaps.

"Yeah, yeah. My point is, he sounds awesome and I want to meet him. Hey, do you think he knows the Doctor? Not the real one obviously, but like, the actor?"

"What?" Jaeli knows exactly what she means, but the best way to change a topic in her house is by getting her niece to jump on a fandom train. She wouldn't shut up for at least a half hour and everyone will be forced to ride along with her. Scott is the first to groan and throw back his head in exaggerated angst over their fate. Serves him right for bullying his little sister.

"The Doctor. Doctor Who, Jaeli. Come on. He sounds a lot like 10. He's my favorite. Did you know, 10 is Scottish in real life? He fakes his accent for the show."

"Right." Jaeli says, smiling to herself. She loved it when a plan came together.

"You think they know each other? Oliver and David Tennant?" Crap. That is not the ramble Jaeli was picturing. When did her love life become more interesting than traveling time and space in a little blue box?

"Oh yeah, I'm sure they do. Scotland's really small."

"What!" Ariel shouted.

"Ari, volume." Her mother mumbled, rolling her eyes and giving up. Jaeli almost feels bad.

"I was just kidding, Ari." The disappointment on her face is almost akin to the *Santa is actually your mom… no not in the Tim Allen way* discussion of Ariel's fourth grade Christmas break. "Sorry."

"You're the worst." Jaeli shrugs it off, she's pretty sure she has heard her niece use that same phrase as a compliment many times before. Catherine takes another cookie to nibble on while she eyes Jaeli and Jaeli can feel her stare on the side of her neck but refuses to look. She knows her sister doesn't believe her. About what specifically she isn't sure, but she is not going to open that can of worms.

CAUGHT IN A LIE

"But seriously, Ariel's right." Catherine says around a gingerbread man's head. "He sounds great, so why aren't you dating him?"

"I don't even know if he's coming back to the States after break. Not for sure really, he's pretty spontaneous." No one seems to be buying it. Jaeli could feel the sweat trickling down her back. Thank God for the absorbency of ugly sweaters. "And really, we're better suited as friends. Long distance is one thing, but dating someone from another country is a bit of a stretch, don't you think? And one of us would have to leave the country every three months or so because of visas and how would either of us hold down a job like that? It would be crazy."

"Unless you got married." Her mother says like it's nothing. "Like me. And your father. No problems."

"You're thinking too far ahead again Jaeli, live for the day." Of course Marianna and all her money problems would say that. "Have a little fun. You can't be bitter about your nonexistent love life if you're married to a career you've barely even started yet."

"Your sister is right. These things, they sort themselves out, like the job. You have a gift Jaejae. School and working these jobs are so stressful for you and you are barely ever home with me now. You could have been a great reader like your grandmother. I'll teach you to read the glass again, yes?"

"She doesn't need to learn parlor tricks if she has the gift mom." Catherine grumbles, flicking nonpareils across the table at her. To her mother's credit, she is completely ignored.

"You could have been a Renai like your father. Then you don't have to worry about staying in one place. You two would travel together like when your father and I first met. You loved the Renaissance Fairs as children. It would be so nice. Ah, how I miss him, your father was so good to us."

"You talk about him like he died." Catherine says, probably suspicious if theire mother knew something they didn't. But Jaeli knew their mother would never keep something like that from them.

"Yeah, he just left with a wench from one of those fairs mom. Literally, probably." Marianna said. She had always been more vocal about her true feelings concerning their father.

"Mhmm, that lifestyle worked out great for a marriage." Catherine tattered back.

"You stop that right now you two. You don't talk about your father that way. He was a good man. Now, Jaeli, what you think? I teach you the glass or do you want to use your father's cards?"

"You know I want to stay in school mom." Jaeli finally snaps, the conversation wearing on her. It seems to be a Christmas tradition. Jaeli's mother looks hurt and it sobers her, she grabs her mother's hand and squeezes. "Maybe later, ok?"

As the night goes on, conversation ebbs away from Jaeli and flows back in with various comments and questions regarding the mysterious Oliver. Her mother seems to blindly approve of everything she says, her trust in Jaeli to speak honestly and be capable to figure all of this out is almost too much. Catherine will occasionally butt in with comments bordering on jealousy and keep trying to disprove what she's said, which of course nudges Jaeli's new lying streak. She's almost starting to worry when Marianna starts to show interest with her probing questions and when Jason follows suit, poking away at the cracks in her story. Jaeli isn't comfortable lying, not like this. It's too much to keep everything interesting while trying to keep her story straight. She thinks they must all be onto her, like the time in first grade when she pretended to have a twin and they played along to tease her, knowing full well she didn't have a twin because they were there when she was born! This lie is just as impossible, but it seems like they're all just genuinely interested and want to meet her new friend.

CAUGHT IN A LIE

When even Scott jumps on the Oliver train, the guilt really sets in. Catherine keeps trying to tell her own story and getting interrupted because of Jaeli. Because of a silly, selfish lie. Why did she even do it? Was it that frustrating and embarrassing that she was a twenty five year old, single, driven woman? It shouldn't be.

Who cares about relationships? Jaeli has never had time for them in the past. Why is it bothering her so much now, to the point where she lets herself fall into this horrible, muddy hole again? Is it because she's boring? Because all she can talk about is homework and professors? *What is wrong with her?*

That glaring, red, compulsive liar comes boldly back to the forefront of her mind and she wants to cry. That couldn't have been about her. She never used to lie. Not like this. Not big ones. Everyone pretends a little sometimes.

"Can you ask him if he knows any famous Scottish people? Like maybe Craig Ferguson or David Tennant or OH! Gerard Butler?" Ariel pipes in again. It's all too much.

"Later Ari, um. I think if you guys don't mind I'm going to go lay down. All those cookies are giving me a stomach ache."

"But you only had a couple."

"A couple too many I guess." Jaeli says with a fake smile. Apparently she can't even be honest about her emotions anymore. "I'm just going to have a quick nap."

She hurries down the hall, not even clearing her place, just needing to be alone for a little while before maybe Oliver wasn't good enough and she starts a lie about winning the lottery or something else equally ridiculous.

She turns off the twinkle lights strung up around her room, Christmas or not, and closes her eyes taking deep breaths to calm down. When she finally falls asleep, she dreams of those familiar blue eyes. But this time the laugh lines around them aren't wrinkled with a smile, they're sad. Maybe even angry.

It feels like they're judging her.

EMILY TALLMAN

***

Soon after New Year's, Ariel has to go back to school so the house is once again left to Jaeli and her mother. She is almost going to miss all the noise and Mud related drama. Almost. She would probably miss the stupid cat the most. That big, matted poof of fur always lying flat on the bottom stair, making these little hunting noises like she isn't the most obvious thing on her mother's cranberry colored carpeting. A little love from her mom at least got all the clumps of mud and God knows what else out of her fur though. Well, at least until the next time it was unleashed on the poor field mice of the neighborhood.

Soon enough it's time for Jaeli to move back to Boston too. She's going to miss home, the easy pace of it and her mother. But she is looking forward to her freedom again. And of course being one semester closer to her goal. If she kept up the work from last semester, she would be graduating a semester ahead of schedule, no problem. The extra hours at Coordinated Counseling Sessions of Rhode Island are a definite help in her two thousand hours too.

With the new semester comes old friends in Trisha and Alexandra and a new friend in Theo, who is Trisha's cousin and Alex's new man since she had spent the holiday bouncing back and forth between her house and visiting Trisha and the Halls. Jaeli sees the healthy new relationship still in its sickeningly sweet stage and gets closer to Trisha while making fun of them. She wants to tell her friends of the "Oliver drama" over break. She wants to tell them none of it was ever real, but this is the first group of people that have stuck with her for so long. Alex isn't even taking the same psych class as she and Trisha this year, opting to switch back to Secondary Education, something she would regret come next semester. Yet, she is still hanging around, still making time in her schedule to stay a part of Jaeli's life.

Jaeli can't do it.

They would forget in time. She won't bring it up anymore even during those awkward moments and soon it would be nothing. Maybe something they can laugh about when they're all life wise and unbothered in a nursing home somewhere, when the big things like a life changing lie are suddenly silly and simple. Jaeli can almost picture it. So she'll stay quiet for now. Who knows if their friendship will even make it to retirement days.

The semester flies by again, guidance counselor sessions becoming less about what classes to take next year and scheduling internship hours and more about a concentration for her thesis. Soon enough, she's forcing herself to study for finals outside the library in the springtime air, thinking about how hard it is to concentrate and how much harder it would be in the summer when people will stroll into the summer classes for their one extra credit smelling like sand, sun block and ocean, ready to jump back into the waves when Jaeli would be taking two more classes that day. It almost makes her regret the decision to take summer classes at all. Why couldn't she stay in school two more years instead of one and a half?

Her phone vibrates on the grass beside her, showing off Catherine's lovely face. That is why. She needs to work, needs to help people. Needs to support herself without loans and credit cards. For herself and to prove to her family that it is possible. She can't be one of the students tanning on the hill next to her, idly taking classes and aiming for the seven year plan. She's wasted enough time with a BA, she wants to finally practice.

"Hey Catherine. I was looking for a distraction from this horrible paper, what's up?"

"What isn't? I'm so sick of this job. If I see one more person with a tan on more than just their driving arm I'm going to scream. I live in the Ocean State! I want to see more beaches and less mandatory overtime."

"At least you get time and a half for it, right?"

"What good is the extra money if I'm too tired to enjoy it? You know what's free fun, Jae? Beaches. Beaches are free and beautiful and I think I'm going to quit my job and buy a beach house."

"That sounds practical." Jaeli watches another girl walk by who thinks it's perfectly fine to attend class in short shorts and a see through top over her bikini and almost sympathizes with Catherine. Normally she'd be defending the girl's right to wear whatever she wants. Today, Jaeli wants to rip the bikini right off of her and high tail it to the nearest pool. "I think I know exactly what you mean."

"Oh yeah, I'm sure campus parties are so stressful for you." Jaeli rolls her eyes. She wouldn't know, she'd never been to one, but her sister needs a punching bag to not go postal at work and she will be one. Or at least try to.

"Have you ever tried to do a keg stand Catherine? It's no easy feet." The sun glares off of her laptop, almost camouflaging the blinking low battery light. Neither is writing a research paper in the summertime apparently.

Six papers, two hundred internship hours and three tests later, she finally gets her beach day. Just one, but it is so lovely she can't care. She doesn't care about the sunburn on her shoulders or that a seagull stole her entire pizza strip or that Catherine complained about it being too hot or Ariel complaining about it being boring, because Jaeli got to nap in the sun while listening to the waves and had wonderful dreams where everything worked out. She wasn't hiding anything from her family or lying to her friends. She was just a woman and she felt loved by the waves caressing her legs, the breeze whispering in her ear and the sun kissing her cheeks. Later she tells her mother the things she had felt and how much fun she had, knowing her mother probably craved good news for once from her daughters as much as Jaeli wished every time the phone rang that her sisters weren't in some sort of crisis. Her mother tells her it is foreshadowing, that she predicted a new man would enter her life before the next full moon. Jaeli laughs, contented and re-freshed.

Three weeks later, the day before the full moon, while she was feeling pulled left and right by new syllabi, family, friends and her own visiting tide she looks up and thinks maybe she needed to give this psychic thing some more credit.

Chapter Five

When Jaeli is four years old she has her first special dream. She dreams of smoke and fire. Snow falls from the sky as an old lady in a nightgown cries. But worst of all are the screams. Screams like she's never heard. Not like when she cries or when her mother yells. The screams are like a wild animal, scary and hurt. She wakes up and runs to her mother's room, shadows in the flames still playing in her mind. Her mother sooths her and lets Jaeli under the covers of her own bed.

In the morning, Jaeli finds her mother in the living room, the news on. A farm is on fire on the screen. A horse ranch. There's a little old lady crying in her pink ruffled nightgown stained with soot. They don't know what happened. She wasn't strong enough to get in the barn and get the horses out. They're gone. Nine horses. White powder falls from the sky around the reporter but it's not snow, its ash. Jaeli's mother reaches out to hold her hand. "I'm so sorry my little Jaebird. I'm so sorry honey."

CAUGHT IN A LIE

***

The second week of school into fall semester, the one where the real work starts and thesis discussion meetings are looming, starts in a whirl. She is so close to her goal, she can taste it! She is tired and overworked and she's pretty sure she sees a picture of herself from last year sleeping in the campus library circling around the internet but she doesn't even care. One more year. Then she will be in the field while she gets licensed. The looming thesis appointment she has nothing to show for can't even get her down today.

She may or may not still be thinking about what her mother said over the summer, and she may or may not have been dreaming of her mysterious nightly visitor that her mind has started referring to as Oliver. Why not? They're the same after all, and both figments of her imagination.

It's been an odd series of dreams, just the two of them sitting together laughing, but she can remember every detail of his face. She guesses it isn't true, that you can't dream of people you've never met. She's never met anyone with so much life in their laughter that their whole body moved and glowed with it and their voice boomed. Has never met anyone with eyes such a dark blue that at first she thought they were brown. Has never met anyone who could put a smile on her face even as her 6:30 AM alarm is blaring and her neck is aching from sleeping wrong. Yet there he is, almost every night now, visiting in higher and higher frequency. Like one morning she will open her eyes and he'll follow her into the waking world. She hopes not. Not if it meant the hooded stranger is real too.

She doesn't care for those particular dreams.

Jaeli won't think of that now though, she'll just try to think how best to word an entire night of laughter and no tidbits of conversation or any other pertinent details for her mom to pick apart or analyze later.

After too many minutes of doodling and no actual dream recording, Jaeli gets on with her morning.

The day continues on in the most mundane way with frustrating undertones. Undertones like forgetting about a Psych 480 assignment she was in the middle of when Catherine had called and that she never got back to. That was certainly frustrating. She can't afford hits to her grades like that. Well, realistically Jaeli can, she just can't make a habit of it. One missed assignment or slept through class a semester is practically inevitable with her workload, she just can't let it touch her GPA and she'll be fine.

When her classes are finally done for the day, she heads over to a little bakery that Trisha has found for them to work on their thesis together. It's conveniently close to Trisha's apartment, but it is also close enough to campus, so Jaeli doesn't complain, even if the walk back in the dark later will be intimidating. She wouldn't have the ground to complain anyway unless she could find a place magically in the middle between their apartments that also had caffeine, Wi-Fi and didn't care if students spent far longer at a table than it would typically take to sip a latté. When Jaeli arrives, she welcomes the coffee and pastry scented blast of A/C to the face as she peeks left and right for Trisha. It doesn't take long to spot the unruly hair with two hands stuck inside of it as her friend glares at a glowing lap top screen.

"Not going well I take it?" Jaeli asks.

"I think I'm going to lose some weight and become an exotic dancer." Jaeli unpacks her bag quietly and waits for her friend to continue, biting back a little grin at what looks like some pink frosting on Trisha's nose. Yup, there is definitely a small stack of cupcake wrappers in danger of being crushed by her friend's elbow. "It's been a weird day, Jae."

"Oh…. Okay, I was thinking that was a perfectly normal thing for you to say but sure. Continue. What's wrong?"

CAUGHT IN A LIE

Trisha hums a giggle Jaeli isn't quite sure is sarcastic, frantic or amused and clears off some more room at the table for Jaeli's work. "It's a good plan though, right? Do you know how much money those people make? And it all takes place at night and school has officially made me nocturnal, so there's that." She takes a chug of coffee, emptying the dregs with a less than impressed face before adding the cup to her pile. "I think it's pretty obvious that this would be the perfect career for me."

"Well with all those valid points, how could you not?"

"I know, right?" Jaeli picks up her friend's pile of cups, plates and wrappers and brings them over to the trash and buss bins, ordering a hot chocolate on her return and a refill for Trisha to give her a little breathing space. When she pushes the vanilla frappe across the table and bends underneath to plug in her laptop, Trisha continues. "I may have writers block to the point of procrastination in the form of reading horrible Buffy the Vampire Slayer fanfiction I wrote when I was in the seventh grade and getting in my head about what a bad writer I am because my 15 day deadline before my meeting with Dr. Zed is quickly approaching and I don't even know what I'm writing anymore after he shot down my fandom as an addiction idea and I'm scared shitless and I can't even—" Trisha takes in a long breath in the form of a frozen slurp, pinching the top of her nose at the resulting brain freeze. "So strippers. Seems like a valid life choice. One I'll look back on with pride."

"When you're not sure where your life is going, stripping is a good gateway career. It can lead to so many opportunities." Jaeli says, sipping her own drink. She should have gotten something cold, but she wanted the sugar.

"It just seemed like the perfect next step."

"Mm. I'm sure there's even some crazy fetish club out there that won't even make you shave your legs in the winter."

"I know you're being sarcastic Jae, but it's probably true." Jaeli nods, opening her own thesis doc with a terrifying amount of page glowing white in its blankness. "That sarcasm of yours is going to confuse your clients one day."

They tap away at their respective keys for a while, what feels like torturous days but was probably only a couple of hours, the tail end of which Jaeli can feel someone starring at them. Maybe it's a worker frustrated about the lost table space or someone judging their not exactly public appropriate conversation. That is, if you didn't know Trisha and her past questionable careers that occasionally sound tempting in the face of intimidating workloads and if they were even here long enough to have heard it.

It's distracting as hell. Jaeli bumps her elbow into Trisha's and nods her head once in the direction the stare is coming from. "I think you already have a client lined up." She mumbles, not wanting to draw attention.

Trisha's head shoots up and Jaeli sighs put upon at the subtlety. "Um, nope. He is definitely looking at you. And now he's approaching. Aw, crap."

"You have frosting on your nose." Jaeli rushes, jamming her face closer to her screen to avoid the unwanted attention. A pair of feet shuffle in front of them and a pair of large hands come down to rest on the empty chair they have both been propping their feet up on.

"You have…just… *unbelievable* eyes. Wow."

It isn't the first time Jaeli has heard a variation of this line and she's sure it won't be the last. It comes with the territory of having one blue eye and one mostly brown. "Heterochromia." She murmurs. "Exciting, I know. Go Google it." She continues tapping away at her barely thought out thesis and puts some serious consideration into the colored contacts Ariel had mentioned over break. She would smile politely at what is surely a gaping, hung over frat bro, but she has found an arched brow and no eye contact is usually more effective at revealing how done she is with a situation. However, when he continues to hover and she finally looks up, Jaeli sees something

CAUGHT IN A LIE

she isn't quite expecting. Something familiar and impossible. She feels her face flush in instant guilt and embarrassment. *Oh no* rushing through her mind followed by, *not again. Not now.*

"Hi. M' names Olli. Uh, Oliver Scott. Mind if I sit?" Trisha gasps dramatically next to her and Jaeli's hands freeze over her keyboard. *This is so bad.*

Shit. Unable to look away from the sure to be train wreck of a man who was never real but was definitely supposed to be dead walking up to her in a bakery like it's nothing. *This is definitely new.*

"You think this is funny? You've got some nerve you little bitch!" Trisha says standing up. She is using that eerie kind of calm voice that broadcasts they would never find his body. Or at least not all of it if he didn't get his shit together right now. "Who the hell put you up to this, 'cause we're about to have words."

"Wha?"

Jaeli has to do something. Has to take action, clear the air. This is so very bad. "Trish, it's not…" But she can't do it. "I mean it's okay. People can have the same name. It's fine. Is that your actual name? Really?"

The man pulls out a foreign ID, a big, white UK inside a blue square at the top left hand corner, and yeah. Unless he works in the DMV and is making IDs for what? Kicks? It was college, she is a grad student in a big city, and it's not like anybody actually knows who she is. This is so very, very bad.

"See? It's fine. Just a weird coincidence."

"*Weird?* I'll say. Kid, you better watch yourself, Oliver Scotts don't –"

"Trish, who's being the bitch now?" Jaeli quickly jumps in before her friend can say more, offense heavy in her voice. She feels bad for snapping like that, but it will protect Trisha in the long run, right?

"Well, I'm just saying. This is fucked up. It's late anyway." Her friend starts shoving things into her bag with quick movements before finally looking back at Jaeli, her face and ears burning hot at having upset her friend and Oliver still hovering. "Are you going to be okay?"

"I'm fine. I'll, uh see you later." Trisha gives Oliver another skeptical look before leaving in a huff.

"Erm... may I ask what that was?"

"Nothing. I wrote a story once about a guy called Oliver. It's nothing." Jaeli says, expelling a breath she didn't know she had been holding. She has a horrible feeling about this. It's probably just guilt.

"Oh yeah? Was he a hero? Dashing, charming?" The man waggles a distinct set of dark ginger eyebrows. "Was it a dirty story?"

"No! God. He was a loser. I killed him off." Jaeli flushes and rings her hands. Why is she so nervous? She hasn't lied to him, just about him. And he isn't going to be around long enough to find out.

"Well that's a bit harsh." He gestures to her cup, swills of cocoa at the bottom gone cold from sitting out for so long. "Need another?" There's that no good, horrible, very bad feeling again.

"Uh—"

"Great. Be right back."

Jaeli drops her head down onto her key board and doesn't pick it up until the sticky key alarm is sounding. A never ending line of *nnnnnnnnnnnnnnnnnnnnnnnnnnnnnnnnnnnnnnnnnnnnnnnnnnnnnnnnnnnn* is making its way down the page.

So far, that is probably the easiest part of her essay to understand. Maybe she should start over.

"You had a hot chocolate? That's adorable."

Jaeli pokes at the bloated marshmallow decorated with a chocolate smile as it melts into her cinnamon hot chocolate. "I don't like coffee."

"Tha's rubbish. You just haven't had good coffee."

"I've had plenty. Enough to know I don't like it."

"Heathen. Fine. Suit yourself."

"I will." A silence forms that Oliver seems content to leave awkward. Too bad Jaeli is uncomfortable enough with social situations to let it stand. Not to mention the strangeness of it all. She takes a sip from the chocolate and lets the sweet, smooth warmth flood through her veins. "Thanks. So... where are you from?"

"Scotland! Thought that was obvious."

"Yeah, no. I got that. I was wondering what part."

"Oh, well, Thurso. It's a little, well not really little, it's pretty busy, but we're a fishing town on the coast." Jaeli's never heard of it. "I know. You've never heard of it. Sorry I can't be from the more romantic Glasgow or Edinburgh but don't worry. You'll fall for me soon enough."

He rambles on while Jaeli wonders if it's possible to drown herself in her oversized coffee cup. You only needed two inches to drown, right? She can do it.

CHAPTER SIX

Jaeli might not get a lot done in the way of a thesis, but she'd be lying if she didn't find the next couple of hours she is forced into spending with the Scot an odd kind of charming. Usually her introversive ways have no patience for this sort of thing, but she lets him bring her pastry samples and refill her drink and even poke at her screen and look through what she's writing, even if all he had to offer was a long sigh and a 'beats me'.

"You're a bright one aren't ya? Thas not my thing really. I'm more of the starving artist type. I'm smart, don't gea me wrong, I got intae Royal academy and I think I'm going tae try a grad program at the Rhode Island School of Design."

"You came all the way from Europe for RISD?"
"No, I came for family, but you've got no pride have ya? RISD's great. Definitely in the top ten art schools and it'd be closer to me sis."

It seems she's started a babble fest about his sister and then his ma and da back across the pond, or loch she guesses. She uses it

47

as background noise while she starts typing again. It's kind of nice, familiar almost. Like she knows him, and she knows why but she doesn't want to think of that. It's just a coincidence. He isn't even that charming and for someone with such an interesting voice, she can't understand half the things he says. Scottish actors in movies were definitely Americanized or maybe Anglicized, because half the words coming out of his mouth, well, aren't. English that is. The word baffie was baffling for one. Soon enough she finds herself squinting at his lips as if that will help her mind translate. He seems to notice and gives a dazzling smile.

"It's not what you think, I just can't understand half, no maybe three quarters of what you're saying."

He throws his head back and groans into his hands, "Well you could hae told me now. Jesus I'm probably gabbing like a fooking bampot." That she mostly got. "So do I need tae start again, did you even get my name or am I just some lousy creep bringing you nibbles?"

Jaeli finds herself genuinely laughing for the first time in a while and even harder at his fallen face. She's a horrible person.

"Fine, go ahea. Laugh. Have a good hoot a' the poor foreigner with no friens." Jaeli bites her lips, she didn't actually want to make the guy feel bad. She isn't even sure if she still wants him to leave. Scratch that, he still very much needs to leave. Just from Trisha's reaction alone, she cannot keep this guy around. Jaeli looks into those familiar eyes though and gets caught. It isn't fair. She looks again at her life and her choices and wishes she could go back and just write a stupid paper about her sisters or never really knowing her dad. Was opening up really that hard? Was taking the easy way out worth all this? "God, I said it already but your eyes are really somethin'. I ain't never seen eyes like those." He looks away, a blush burning splotchy red under his freckles. "Oh I'm an idiot."

This is going to hurt. She knows it will, but for some reason she agrees to meet him for coffee again the next day. Not as a date, she makes that very clear. Just to see some of his art, eat some more free pastry, sip some chocolate and have him take another look at her thesis. She's sure Trisha wouldn't mind. She hopes.

***

"Excuse me, you're doing what?"

"I know. I'm insane. Thank you for the observation. But, I don't know. He played the no friends card, Trish. What was I supposed to say?"

"Um, no? It's not that hard. Or you could have just let me scare him away earlier. That would have solved a lot here."

Jaeli deflates a little. This is a bad idea. A bad idea of epic proportions. A bad idea on scale with the bad idea of writing *that* paper. The one she doesn't even have to name because you know the one. *That* one, the one that started all this. And then there's the bad idea of telling her family her dream whatever he was is real. Getting to know this guy is right up there with both of those ideas. Maybe even exceeding in badness because this one would actually affect her life. Secret, sure, they're bad. Lies, the same. But no one would ever have to know. It's kind of hard to keep an actual, living, very talkative and social person to herself. Maybe she could be honest with him? No, that would be a disaster. "Maybe if he is the creep you think he is you can scare him away tomorrow?"

"Do your dirty work for you?"

"More like protect me and walk me home in the dark if he's a psycho? Provide numbers for me? So I don't look like prey to the inner serial killer you think he possesses."

Trisha lets out another loud sigh from her soul into the phone but ultimately agrees as long as she actually gets help with her thesis instead of a bitch fest and if she can invite Theo for muscle. Her words, not Jaeli's.

CAUGHT IN A LIE

Jaeli's Tuesday is typical, two classes, her short day, followed by some internship hours and a quick meet up with her therapist from last semester. She decides not to mention the big shocker from the day before until after the meet up tonight. She's sure the next month will come up with plenty of other things to relay in the mandatory sessions.

Soon enough, it's four and she is meeting Trisha, Alex and Theo in the bakery. She notices Oliver right away, it was hard to miss the shock of red hair, big smile and bigger wave. Maybe she's stereotyping but she thought Scottish guys were the strong silent type. That was probably just when they were concentrating on not letting the wind sweep up their kilts. Maybe they're just more social in a good ol' pair of Levi's. He doesn't appear to be expecting her so soon if his reaction is anything. He rushes into the back while she walks over to her friends and sets up her things at their table.

"That was him I take it?" Alex side eyes her, raising a pierced brow in a look that's anything but impressed.

"Guess I' not hallucinating then." Jaeli jokes. Her friends are not amused. Oliver takes that moment to slam down a thick, black portfolio.

"Here we have it. They're just photos. Commissions an' things I did at home an' in New York. Donnae show my real work tae people I just met. No offense."

Alex looks like she's won over, other eyebrow going up to join the first and lips pursing. Theo pinches her arm and she punches his lightly. "Eh, so thas it really. Whatcha workin on then? Same thing?"

Jaeli turns her lap top to face him. "Aw, you got rid of that key smash bit. I liked that bit, only part I really understood if I'm bein' honest. You sure you want tae write about this rubbish?"

"The health care system marginalizing mental illness is rubbish?"

50

EMILY TALLMAN

"No, but well, it's not exactly exciting." Jaeli's eye twitches, frankly Oliver is lucky lasers didn't fly out of it. "Nae like that, thas not what I meant. Erm, just. Maybe write something you care about more. More than you obiously do this. I'm doin it again aren't I? Bein' a bampot? I just meant that, maybe write about what you want tae do with your career. What makes you different? Everybody's going tae go for the topical approach, ain't they? Be different. Stand out. They might just put you in the papers."

Jaeli's a little speechless, luckily Trisha is able to help with that. "Guess I'm officially changing my thesis then. Tell me Oliver, what path do you think I should take with psychiatry?"

"Well dea ya like art? Art therapy's great. Learn a lot about a person by how they portray the world. Now if ya excuse me, I am still on the clock and that horrible missus Berkley's givin me the hell eyes again. Can I get you lot some bevies? I know you want a hot chocolate you fool, what about the rest of ya?"

The rest of the evening goes smoothly, Oliver bouncing between work and their table and starting to grow on her friends. Trisha seems to take his idea to heart and restarts her research. At least it's only September, all the power to her. Jaeli isn't quite so convinced she should change directions yet. Especially since that warm, charming quality Oliver had yesterday is starting to wear on her today.

She can't really explain it, but she feels threatened. Like she's being backed into a corner. Maybe she brought her friends here hoping they wouldn't like him, that they'd have the reaction Trisha had yesterday. They didn't. And Jaeli is ready to leave.

"I'm starving. What about you guys?" She asks on one of Oliver's flits back to the counter.

"I get off in 30 if ya donnae mind waiting."

"Sure thing." Trisha mumbles around a pen, eyes enraptured on her screen. "You know, I think this is exactly what I needed. Fresh start and this art therapy stuff is really interesting. I kinda scoffed at the class synopsis I read last year, but maybe I'll check it out next semester. Ooh! Maybe I can audit this semester. It's only the second week right? There should be drops soon I might be able to snatch." Oliver laughs and continues making his coffee while Jaeli rolls her eyes and sighs. *Great.*

They wait the thirty minutes while Jaeli's writer's block continues in the distraction of her friends finding their friggin' paths in life and laughing at Oliver's stupid slang.

They end up in a pizza joint a couple blocks over from the theater were Theo is an assistant stage manager. If anything can cheer her up it's a nice sugary coke and some melty cheese, and this place has some awesome cheese. One thing she could agree with Oliver about today. They end up closing the restaurant with all their talking and leave a big tip for grad students for holding up the table. At least their waitress wouldn't spit in their food when they definitely come back. Jaeli wishes they'd deliver as far away as her apartment, but she doubts it. Is it bad to consider moving just for a pizza place? Theo and Alex split from their little group to head home, leaving Jaeli with a drowsily stumbling Trisha and a loud Oliver, still talking about the amazing food. She can't blame him. He leads the way, swinging his portfolio about as he talks, checking a street sign before heading into an alley almost half a block ahead of them. Another thing she can put on the list of things she didn't really care for about real Oliver, he wasn't considerate of slow walkers like Trisha or aware enough of his surroundings to even realize he was leaving them in the dust.

She hears a scuffle up ahead and jumps, clutching Trisha's arm with eyes wide. She hears Oliver yell something and what sounds like a fight. Shit, this can't seriously be happening.

Jaeli runs to the head of the alley where she sees a girl, no more than sixteen slam Oliver into a wall. Seriously? Was he chivalrous or stupid?

"Hey!" Jaeli yells at the girl charging for her, wallet and art in hand. "Give me back the folio and the wallet and I'll give you a twenty. Trust me kid, it's more than that shitty artwork will get you and definitely more than he has in his wallet. We're grad students."

The girl tries to duck around her but Trisha catches her arm. "Don't make me fight you kid, don't you know grad students have nothing to lose? You're lucky we haven't beaten the crap out of you and left you for the pigs." Trisha could make a point when she needed to. The girl slams the stuff on the ground and takes off, smart enough not to wait for the cash. "Promising money, you idiot! What if she had a knife or something?"

"You're the one that actually grabbed her. And you! You can't even take a little girl?" Jaeli yells at Oliver who's slumped against the wall before she realizes he isn't really moving.

"Oh shit."

"Oh my God. Oliver!" Jaeli yells. She slams her knees on the pavement when she rushes towards him, slapping his cheeks and watching his eyes flutter at her. When she's satisfied that they're open enough, she checks the back of his head. There is definitely blood. "Oliver, hey. Are you okay? Can you walk?"

"You really think my art is shite?"

"That's what you're taking away from this?" He gives her imploring eyes more suited to a puppy. "I wouldn't have saved it if I did. Now get up. She probably has friends she's working with close by and it would be stupid to stay. Can you walk? I think we might need an ER."

Oliver pushes himself to his feet if a little sideways and palms the back of his head, taking his hand away to look at the blood. It isn't exactly dripping, but there's a lot of blood. "Nah. Think it's just scraped. Well, this was all embarrassing." He stumbles for a couple steps before Trisha and Jaeli fit themselves under an arm each and walked him out onto the street.

CAUGHT IN A LIE

"You know any urgent cares nearby? Do you think they'd let us on a train if he's bleeding?"

"Told ya I dinnae need it dammit. Let go, I'm not even hurt. I hit my hea not mi legs woman." Jaeli scoffes and moves away from his side, his body follows her, knees buckling. Trisha protests the extra weight and Jaeli rushes to support him again.

Jaeli sighs and stays put while Trisha opens up Google maps, Oliver content to rest his head back and squint up at the street lights.

"S'a braw bricht moonlicht nicht the nicht." He mumbles, brogue thick enough that she has no idea if those are even words.

"Yeah, you definitely did more than scrape your head."

"Wha? No. It's a sayin'. The sky, the moon, can't really see the stars but s'nice.

"Okay buddy. Come on." Trisha says, holding the phone out in front of them and checking the streets for which way their little dot is supposed to be moving.

"Ha. Thirty Fourth Street. You're my miracle on thirty Fourth Street. Rose will love tha. I'm not even in New York and I'm still living the dream more than her."

Jaeli freezes and Trisha side eyes her as Oliver stumbles at the sudden halt. "Let's get you some help. You sure you're good to walk or you want to try for the next cab?"

They end up taking a cab and then waiting while Oliver gets a couple staples, the sound of the gun making Jaeli flinch each time. For not being able to take down a little girl, she has to give Oliver props for not even seeming phased by staples being put into his head and gravel scrubbed out of it. Trisha looks like she's dying to ask the dreaded "are you okay?" but thankfully it never comes up. She declines an invite to sleep over Trish's that night after they see Oliver back to his apartment over the bakery, needing to get home. As soon as she's through the door she goes to her laptop and filters through her assignment folders looking for one in particular.

It's not possible.

EMILY TALLMAN

***

Jaeli Tal
Writing 220 – Creative Writing
Professor Christopher Jacobs
September 3, 2011

Assignment One
 It was like any other day, the same boring routine. A future yesterday. The sun rose above the trees outside the bay window of my bedroom, sending a harsh beam of light through the cracks not enveloped by the thick, white shade. I rolled over uncomfortably and reached blindly for the alarm clock to check the time. My tired eyes focus on the glowing red numbers – 6:23. I would wake up an hour early again. Damn the sun. I try to roll over and throw a pillow over my head, but it's no use, the phone rings. I swing my feet out from under my soft cotton sheets and press them to the cold, hard wood floors. Taking my time, I reach the phone just as the answering machine picks up. "Hey, you've reached Jaeli. Sing your song at the beep and if it's pretty, I'll ring later." The ominous beep proceeded and I waited for one credit card company or another to start their persistent early morning pitch. I swear, if they didn't start calling at a reasonable hour, but then the voice caught me by surprise.
 "Hey Jae, how does this sound? Happy Birthday to you… Happy Birthday to—"
 I fumbled to answer the phone only to knock it to the floor. I picked it up quickly to hear my best friend Oliver laughing.
 "Olli? What are you doing calling at" I spun around, twisting the cord around me to look back at the clock, "6:30 in the morning!"
 "I wanted to be the first to wish you a happy birthday. Was I the first?"

CAUGHT IN A LIE

"As a matter of fact, the sun beat you by seven minutes."

"Damn, I guess next year I'll have to call at midnight." He laughed. "But seriously, how was it? Good right? American Idol material?"

"Ha! Don't quit your day job."

"How could I with a minx like you coming in everyday to sate her chocolate addiction. I'd be insane to give up our little lunch chats."

"Yeah, yeah, so funny. Well, I better start getting ready or I'll miss our little lunch chat." I said grinning to myself. I loved flirting with him. It was so easy and he always played back, but at the end of the day, we would always be just friends and occasionally 'plus one's' for each other.

"Well, I wouldn't want to be responsible for that. I'd have to leave early and come searching for you. Oh, Jaeli baby, how would life go on?"

"Stop! I'm hanging up. Goodbye Olli. You'll see me at 2PM on the dot."

"I had better, don't you dare be late."

"I'll try my best, but don't do anything drastic if I am. See you later."

"Sooner I hope. Oh, and Jae?" A few seconds passed before he continued in a voice suddenly very serious, "Happy Birthday, I love you." And he hung up. Well, that was different. I stood there with the phone to my ear, listening to nothing while I contemplated what that meant. Surely it was just a friendly thing. But what if it wasn't? No, I had long snuffed such notions of anything forming between myself and Olli. He was a 10 and I was barely a 3. Olli was funny, outgoing, adventurous, and lord was he gorgeous. 6'2", light red hair, broad shoulders and eyes such a dark blue from a distance, you'd swear they were brown. Still, was it possible? Could a person like Oliver Scott be interested in me? No, we were just friends. It was a mistake.

EMILY TALLMAN

I undressed and made my way to the adjoining bathroom. I wouldn't think about this anymore. I would pretend like it never happened. I'm sure I heard him wrong, and if the 'L' word was in anyway used, it was with friendship in mind, obviously.

I continued through my morning routine, concentrating more than necessary on the usual tasks until the clock finally showed that it was eight and time to leave.

After a long day of Gen-Eds and watching the snow flurry down through the windows, it was time for my four hour break with office hours in the student union before my psych class. I still had about a half hour before I would need to replace Jackson in the Psych club office in the student union, so I made my trudge through the slush two blocks down to the good café off Hemenway Street.

I stomped the dirty, New England winter mush off my boots and got in out of the cold. The scent of the bakery was already a blast of energy to my tired brain cells as I strode up to the counter for my daily cup of cocoa. While I waited for the steaming mug to warm my hands against, I peered over the counter and tried to look into the back for my pastry decorator and waiter.

Olli walked by the door and smiles his classic crooked smile through the little glass square, he was brandishing a cupcake, probably a lemon one, my favorite, and holding up a finger telling me to wait. What else could I do? He made small talk with the cashier on his way over, stealing my hot chocolate to deliver himself. He took a step my way and then turned on his heel to retrieve something from under the counter. A single long stem rose the bright red color of a ripe strawberry. He continued my way and pulled me into a hug. "Happy birthday." He said, breaking away, careful not to spill the hot drink. My heart skipped a beat as his eyes meet mine. Stop thinking it, *I tell myself,* you don't love him. *But who wouldn't think she was in love with him? He had thrown the 'interesting European student card down day one and had been breaking hearts with it, mine included, I'm sure. "You, my dear, are two minutes late. I nearly*

CAUGHT IN A LIE

went frantic. I had to amuse myself with the lovely new Lisa, who is apparently my manager's 'sister'." He chuckles and finger quotes. Olli loved to poke fun at the sorority girls that thought they owned the little shop every time they stopped by.

"Well, then. I suppose she's off limits." He offered his arm and I took it, we made our way to the chilly little table in the corner that everyone avoided in winter, but we liked for the fresh air.

"That normally wouldn't mean anything, but I don't care about her. So I guess she's safe." I had no idea what to say, I just sat and stared at his smiling profile. He put my cup down and turned to me. "Have you eaten lunch?"

"Not yet but I have to head back to the office. You take your break yet?"

"Lisa tell your sister I'm going on break, be back in 45!" Olli shouted, much to the distress of the little old ladies from the brownstones across the street enjoying their daily coffee, gossip, and community newspapers they were guaranteed to 'forget' they didn't bring to the bakery with them and take home later.

I rolled my eyes at his antics and waited as he ran back to the kitchen to drop his apron and no doubt filch us some lunch. I brushed the petals of my birthday rose and took a subtle sniff. It almost smelled like pineapple, meaning he probably took this from someone's fancy order. I'm sure they wouldn't miss one rose. I had never gotten flowers… or a flower *before so I wasn't going to complain.*

He came back flaunting two paper bags, food filched indeed, and we headed brusquely back to campus with red cheeks and freezing fingers. When we got up to the hall with the student offices, Olli hung back to poke at the contents of the bags as if he didn't know what was inside while I went to relieve Jackson so he could do whatever it was he did when he wasn't pretending not to smoke out the window. When she walked into the office however, Jackson wasn't quickly shoving a butt into a soda can, but jamming a card back into a bouquet of roses instead.

"Uh, they're for you. Didn't know it was your birthday Jae. You want me to cover your office hours?"

"No... that's alright. Thanks though." Jaeli cautiously approached the flowers, pulling out the slightly crinkled card and read the birthday wish with some skepticism. "Jackson? You didn't, did you?" I asked with narrowed eyes at the grad student trying to rush his way out. You probably shouldn't hold flowers like a sword, but what the hell did you actually do with the things?

"Nope. I'm with Abby. You know, from accounting club? Remember?"

"Right. Well, see ya Monday I guess." She smiled, still pointing the roses at him as he left. Olli finally made his way into the office and raised his eyebrows at the threatening way I was holding the bouquet.

"Erm...everything okay?"

"Apparently I have a secret admirer. It's weird. You don't think someone is silence of the lambs-ing psych students do you? Is this an intimidation thing? Or a joke maybe?"

"Probably somebody's just trying to do something nice for you. Here, he held out a bag. Sit, eat, I'll go find the offending things some water."

He left looking a little upset and I couldn't blame him. I griped about my single status enough that he was probably worried what kind of creep would send flowers too. Or maybe he was annoyed I wasn't as appreciative as a future spinster should be? But screw that, it's weird that I don't know who this guy, or girl even, could be. And creepy. At least they weren't delivered to one of my morning classes.

I opened the bag to find half a Panini and the lemon cupcake. The cupcake had an adorable marshmallow snowman on top of its frosty blue and white buttercream frosting, complete with chocolate buttons, scarf and a carefully dotted smile. I removed it from the bag and set it down to dig into the sandwich when Olli came back and stuck a little pink birthday candle in it.

"Happy birthday!"

"So you've said multiple times today." I glared at him and added a wink for good measure. "Thank you."

"Mm, of course. So, have you got any plans?" He asked, digging into his own lunch.

"Not yet. Why, have something in mind?"

"Well, I was thinking you and me, tomorrow morning, getting on a train and going to New York. You've never seen the sights, I've never seen the sights, we can buy—"

"I don't know." I cut him off. For all that Olli was kind and funny, he never really took into consideration other people's financial situations. "I have a paper due Monday and some research I should start. Finals are soon..."

"I'm hearing a lot of excuses and not any actual answers. Would tickets to Wicked *change your mind?"*

"Let me think about it? It's a lot of money to spend on such short notice and I'd have to take time out of work."

"Sorry, didn't I mention? Trip's on me. It's your birthday, you're not paying for anything."

"I definitely can't accept that."

"Would it make you feel better if I said that by 'me' I meant 'my parents'? The parents you've met on Skype and who think you're adorable and feisty and want you to come live with them? Actually, I'm pretty sure it's a present from them entirely and I need to get you a souvenir while we're there just from me so I'm not such a horrible friend."

Lunch was a little stilted after that. We shared shy smiles as if we hadn't been friends for two and a half years and did homework, Olli picking my brain about a class I had taken last semester that he was in now. Soon his forty five minutes were up and he was heading back to the café, leaving me feeling a little guilty but also to research my paper in peace.

I had just gotten into the meat of the theory I had to look up when I was surprised to hear a knock at the open office door. Walkins weren't unheard of but were pretty rare outside of finals week. I looked up to see a tall, thin man in a navy jumpsuit with light green elegant writing on his shoulder.

"Jaeli Tal?" He asked, eying the roses Olli had put into a plastic cup of water and carefully balanced against in the corner where the desk met a bookcase.

"Yes?" I replied cautiously. He stepped back into the hall and returned with a vase of yellow roses, twice as many as the first bouquet. Oliver's lonely red rose had been outshined again; I wondered how he would take it. I stood up and met the man at the door to take the vase and put it next to the other. "Thank you." I said and he left. I later wondered if I should have left him a tip, I lacked the experience here.

Flowers for the third time in one day, though it was under strange circumstances, I was guilty of feeling quite pleased with myself. It was a nice feeling, hopefully one that would last and not lead to being made into a skin suit or someone's winter preserves. I almost wanted to call home, but I wanted to know who sent them before I got my mother's hopes up that flowers meant a wedding and hordes of new grandchildren. I dug through the flowers in search of a card and eventually found a small yellow heart. "From your secret admirer. I hope you like roses. Make sure you are in your office in an hour." It said in typed letters. Who could this be? I wasn't sure if I wanted to be on campus anymore, let alone in the psych office at that time, what was going to happen? But I didn't have to worry for too long, because right at four a shorter man in a familiar jump suit knocked at my door and delivered three dozen pink roses with a little pink heart reading, "make some room on that cluttered desk, and be there at five. No offence of course."

CAUGHT IN A LIE

I was stunned, but did as the note said and started filing or shredding the piles of paper cluttering the desk only to be inter-rupted at five by a woman in the same jumpsuit and four dozen or-ange roses with a little orange heart that said see you after psych. I was very glad that there would at least be witnesses and even Oliver there to fend off a stalker if needed. He shouldn't mind, the first time we met, I had saved him from a mugger. Well not really him, but his wallet. I had heard shouts from an alleyway by the café and was prepared to call for help, but when I saw a man running toward me with a wallet I decided sticking out my foot may work a little faster. Olli soon caught up and treated me to lunch after calling the police about an unconscious thief on Thirty Fourth Street. It was an inter-esting introduction, definitely one I would never forget.

Shana thankfully got to the office to relieve me a bit early so I had time to haul my roses across campus to the student parking lot and fill my back seat. At least I would know tonight no one was hid-ing in my car, they'd never fit with all the flowers.

I end up making two trips and even with the extra few minutes I barely get to class in time to take my seat in front of Olli. He was a middle isle dweller, looking like he was paying attention but actually being a social media troll behind me, the front row queen trying to get as many participation points as possible. At least I still beat the flower delivery man who knocked just as the professor was beginning the evenings lecture.

"Jaeli Tall?"

"It's Tal." I mumbled slouching in my seat and lifting my hand in a little half-wave." The professor raised an I can wait (not really, I'm a teacher and I'll remember this when reading your next paper) *eyebrow and waited as I took the massive white bouquet and gave a shy smile to the delivery man and a mumbled thanks before slouching further and covering my red face.*

The professor rolled his eyes at the interruption but continued the lecture as I stewed in my embarrassment. I heard Olli chuckle behind me and gave him my best subtle death glare.

"What's all this?" He asked the second the professor started putting away his notes. I let out a deep sigh.

"I honestly don't know. You didn't do it, did you?"

"Jae, sweetheart, I couldn't afford to." That I knew was a lie, he practically had money to burn. He was one of those trust fund assholes that picked up a part time, minimum wage job for the 'character building' and ate his wages away while working. But I thought if it was him, he would want credit so I let it go. I hefted up the huge vase and balanced it on my hip as I dug out my keys and headed back to the parking lot. He followed and soon matched my pace.

"Looks like you have some admirer." He said in a mocking tone.

"I'm not blind, but why?"

"You are blind if you have to ask. Why did you think it was me?"

"Well...I don't know." I didn't want to bring up the phone call this morning, but I had never been anything but honest with Olli, "What you said before you hung up this morning...did I hear you right?"

"You mean when I said I love you?"

"Yeah, that bit."

"I was afraid you had heard that." He sighed. I knew I should have kept my mouth shut." I waited patiently for further response but none came. When we were out in the quad I went to ask and he beat me by saying, "Wait until we're in the car." I did. Once we were seated in my dusty little ford, the perfume of the flowers thankfully covering the stale fast food aroma that haunted most college students, I opened my mouth to ask again, and again he beat me. "I meant it. I've wanted to say it for a long time, and I was going to wait until dinner tonight, but it slipped out. I'm sorry."

CAUGHT IN A LIE

My heart stopped, this better not be a birthday joke. "There's nothing to apologize for. It's fine."

"You don't feel the same way." He said, looking away. He looked too hurt to be joking. Not for the first time, I wondered if anyone had ever told Olli 'no'. "I don't want to hurt our friendship."

I picked at my keys, taking time starting the car, turning up the heat and the radio down low enough where we could still talk, buying myself time to think. I stayed quiet while I remembered our past. The day we met, I felt light headed when I first saw him. That whole lunch my heart nearly beat out of my chest that such an attractive man was paying any attention to me, I thought it was fate. Somehow, when we found out we went to the same school, were interested in the same path of study and started eating lunch together a friendship had formed, but never anything more. Still, that didn't stop the way I felt when I was around him. That dizziness and knee buckling sensation, like I was falling. I suddenly realized why fairy tales call it 'falling in love'. That light headed feeling you get when you finally let go of reason and believe something so wonderful can happen to you feels indeed like dropping off a cliff. I look up to see Olli staring at me, the headlights of a passing car touch his face, highlighting his cheek bones and a piece of his hair that had fallen over his forehead. My fingers twitch with the want to push it back. He looks a little pale, like he may be feeling his guts dropping out of him in freefall too. "I think I do."

"What? Do what?"

"Love you." But a plow drove by drowning my words. Maybe it was a sign that I shouldn't say anything.

"What?" He asked, leaning forward. I blushed and raised my eyes to look at his hands fumbling with something. "This was so embarrassing." I said as I nodded at the back seat full of flowers. I dug through the white bouquet looking for another little note but I couldn't find one. Maybe it had blown away. Olli cleared his throat

and handed me a white heart. 'surprise!' it said in his messy scrawl instead of the inky typed letters of the ones from earlier.

"It wasn't my intention to embarrass you. I remember you saying that you had never received flowers before so I thought what the hell. Only thing is, I didn't know your favorite color so I decided to buy them all. You weren't supposed to figure out it was me until after you got home."

"Why, what's at home?"

"Well, you'll just have to wait and see birthday girl." He sighed again. "I was also hoping this would soften you up so you would go out to dinner with me later. And maybe New York this weekend."

"Well that plan worked. I'd love to go out to dinner with you." It was so much easier to use the L word when not putting I in front of it or you after.

I maneuvered the slushy streets home, Olli oddly silent next to me. He said he didn't want to ruin our friendship, and I hoped that this didn't. Just suddenly everything went from floaty and perfect to incredibly awkward. I should have said it back. Friggin' plows, it wasn't even snowing hard. We hefted the vases out of the back and made the stairs up to my dinky little off campus apartment. We reached the top to see mixed bouquets of peach, purple, light pink, and last but not least, one dozen antique colored roses with a little plush honey colored teddy bear holding a red 'Happy Birthday' balloon. "Jesus Christ Olli, did you buy out the store!"

"I told you, I didn't know what color! And they were all nice!" He was yelling but smiling through it, it was nice to see that smile after the awkward silence. He seemed to be reading my mind and he let a little laugh escape and then another until he was full on clutching his stomach and had to set his flowers down.

"Oh God, I'm a sappy piece of shit. How did this even happen? What the hell did you do to me Jaeli?"

CAUGHT IN A LIE

I almost dropped the ones in my arms when I saw my door covered in little colored hearts, each one holding only one word. Happy – Birthday – Jae. Will – You – Join – Me – For – Dinner – Tonight? Meet – Me — Where – We – First – Met. – There – Will – Be – Another – Present – In – It – For – You. Love – Oliver.

I couldn't believe it. The pink Love heart stood out amongst the others. I struggled to unlock the door and let us in. "How did you do all this?" I asked him as he set down the flowers he was carrying on the counter.

"I came before lunch." He shrugged. "So, which color was your favorite?"

"There are too many to choose from, why don't we bring them all in and I'll try to pick."

"That was my plan from the start." He laughed, took the car keys I gave him and left to get the rest. I turned to set my vases on the kitchen table by the sliding door, and that's when I noticed the mud on my rug...and the glass...there was a hole in the sliding door to the fire escape, right near the handle...the screen was on the ground outside. My pulse rang in my ears, this was wrong, where was Oliver? I didn't want to be alone. I left the room and headed towards the spare bedroom where I kept some sports equipment there thinking this year I'd have time to exercise. I knew I had an aluminum bat somewhere. I opened the door to be met with a hooded stranger. I gasped in a breath to scream but he raised a gun to my face and whispered eerily clear.

"Not a single sound." I was terrified. I had never felt so helpless in my entire life. The best day I had ever had rapidly turned to the worst and then nosedived lower when I heard the click of my front door open. Oliver was back. "Get in." The man said leaning into my face, he put the gun to my chest. I could feel the barrel press against my thin sweater, the cold seeping right through to my sweating skin. My vision started to cloud and I heard Oliver's voice.

EMILY TALLMAN

"Jae, where are…what the—" The stranger shoved me hard against the wall. I woke up to the sound of thudding and scuffling. I lift my head to see Olli and the man rolling on the floor. There is a bang, and another. I can't take my eyes off the two still forms on the floor staring at each other. I can't blink, I can't breathe. The man gets up and runs out the door. Olli leans back against the rug, there's red on him. I crawl over and lean over him. Two spots are spreading over his shirt, on his stomach and on his chest. I scream and gulp in air. Too much, it feels like fire in my lungs. I scream again and again. Olli puts his hand on my face and I stop. Everything is so quiet.

"Call…." He says. I shove my hand into my pockets and rip out my cell phone.

I pound in the numbers and wait what feels like an eternity before I hear, "911, what's your emergenc—"

"Hello, he's been shot. Twice. Help please send help we need an ambulance please!" I shout out my address into the phone and drop it on the floor. The woman continues to talk but I ignore it. I go back to Oliver. "Olli, Oliver please answer me!" He gasps as I try to put pressure on the wounds like they do on TV and he screams through clenched teeth. I pull my hands back. They're covered in his blood, stained red. I can't stop looking at them. I feel his hand on my face again and look back at his. He's so pale and his eyes are darker than they should be, lids heavy and it's scarier than all the blood.

"Jae, please… It's okay… Calm down, I hear the sirens… it's okay."

"What sirens, I don't hear them yet."

"It's okay, come here." He whispered, he pulls my face towards his and pressed his lips to mine. I tasted the blood on his mouth. "I love you, Jae. …I love you so much."

"I hear the sirens now, they're coming Oliver." I said through tears.

CAUGHT IN A LIE

"I love you." He kissed me again and then his hand fell away, his lips stilled, he leaned back to the floor, eyes closed. He's dead! He's dead! *Was all I could think. Two men came running through the door, I jumped, but they were just the EMT's. They crowded Olli. They took him away. They left me on the floor, red on my hands, with the police. The police took me to the hospital. Oliver is in surgery. People milled by me, and when it felt like everything had stopped, I looked up to see that time had flown. A doctor approached me, Oliver is out of surgery, and he is being moved to the Intensive Care Unit.*

"Is he awake?" I asked through more tears as I stood up and prepared to find his room.

"No…" He said it as if there was more to the story. I fell, my knees hit the floor hard, but it was nothing compared to the stinging of tears in the back of my throat and the empty ache in my chest.

Eventually I found my way to his room. I stayed for hours, holding his hand. Telling him every story I could think of about the two of us. "I don't know what more to say Olli. You are so much better at telling stories than I am. I'm probably keeping you asleep."

I closed my eyes and could picture him smiling at me, laughing, exuberantly telling me about one of his adventures until all I can see is the hooded man's face as the gun fires again. I let out a sob and rested my eyes on his face again. To see so much life reduced to such stillness broke every last shard of my heart. "Oliver, I… Olli I suppose that… if it's my last chance to say it that I—" A beeping cut off my words. I had a flash of déjà vu and thought of my answering machine this morning when he sang me 'Happy Birthday' but this beeeeep didn't stop. People started rushing into the room. Machinery was pulled over to him and someone closed the curtains.

They can't save him. He's dead. Everything happened so fast, and I realized that there can't ever be a happy ending because that's not the real end of the story. All stories end in tragedy because eventually everybody dies even if they were loved. And isn't that like falling too?

Olli fell when he was shot. When Olli is pronounced dead, I fell to the ground. I heard him say he loved me five times, he never heard those words from me. I had the perfect relationship with the man I loved. I loved him and he didn't have to love me back, but when he did, it tipped the scales. I felt so good that something had to come take it away and put balance back into the world.

CHAPTER EIGHT

"**Y**ou tell me you dream of him. Every night. That's he your friend and he makes you happy. Then you tell me he's not real and then that he is. Jaejae." Her mom says, voice shaking. Jaeli pinches the bridge of her nose tight, clenching her eyes closed and pinning the phone to her ear. She deserves whatever reaction her mother has. "I don't know what to do with you. You are breaking my heart. Why would you lie like that? Why would you do that?"

Jaeli swallows the thick pain burning the back of her throat. "You guys are always pressuring me to have more, be more. It's like you expect so much from me just going to college. But a Bachelor's degree isn't enough today. I proved that, and it won't get me where I need to be and you all think going back to school is stupid. I just wanted to show you I was normal. That I could be strong and be *something*. Something more."

"Jaejae, a man does not make you more!" Her mother scolds. "Honey, why you think you're not normal? You are you and that is beautiful. I just want you to be happy. That's all. And I think that even if you don't want to admit it, these dreams and this man are proof to you that you have the gift, chav."

"Married and pregnant isn't always happy mom."

"No it is not. But a little family can be. And then you could be settled and have someone to look after you. I don't like that you're alone so much. That's all. You need family. Even if it is just friends."

"Oh I have it. Too much of it most of the time. I move away and I still can't escape it. If a single day goes by when the end of Mari's or Catherine's world isn't spewing at me from the other end of the phone, I'll think you're all dead! They don't get it, that I'm trying to move my life forward. All they do is pull me back into their bull shit. Well I'm sick of it. Maybe I wanted something of my own to talk about for a change. Maybe even just something good, because God knows, there's no such thing as good in our lives." Jaeli ends her rant with a heavy breath and instantly feels the pang of regret in her chest. Her mother doesn't call her with those things, and her sisters try not to worry her. Jaeli didn't need to break that magical dome over her head. "I'm sorry mom, I didn't mean—"

"I didn't know we were such a bother Jae. We just miss you. I will talk to them. We will leave you alone." The sentences are short and cold. Tears slip down Jaeli's cheeks but it's too late now, she can feel it.

"No, mom that's not what I want."

"I think it is. Right now at least. I think that *you think* you know what you want but really you have no idea and that's okay. Fixing problems for you, that's safe Jaeli. That's why you went back to school. What I think is that you should really learn to use your mind. Ok. I go now. You come to us when you're ready. Don't forget your home."

The line goes dead and Jaeli places her phone on the bed next to her. It has been a day. She'd gotten home late, read and reread

CAUGHT IN A LIE

that horrible paper that stared it all and stayed up worrying all night. Any time she lets her eyes slip closed she would start to see his face again and jolt awake. She just wants help, someone to talk to. Telling her mother had been a mistake. It just brought pain to both of them.

She is so selfish.

She catches up on assignments at home and calls out sick from her appointment to observe a session with Dr. Brouche. She just needs a day. One mental health day to figure out what the hell she's doing. Mainly about Oliver and how that is about to throw her entire life off balance, especially since her friends like him so much.

She takes a beat to think. Would it really? Did the two Olivers have to exist as two different entities? Could she just ignore the first and embrace the second? Could she pretend that FakeOliver never existed? It shouldn't be hard seeing as he didn't. But what if RealOliver ever found out? Could she tell him the truth, but no one else? Could she let her friends lie to him and him see her as this broken thing who went through a nonexistent tragedy and was probably broken as far as the dating world was concerned? Did she even want to date him? Isn't she getting a little ahead of herself?

Very. Very ahead of herself. She doesn't even like him. He's loud and obnoxious. Nothing like her dreams. Aside from those eyes anyway, and how important are eyes in a person?

She gets a text from Trisha asking if she is alright and if she needs notes from class. She sent back a quick **fine** and **yes plz** before she eyes the little smiley face with its stupid dash nose that Oliver had sent her last night when they all exchanged numbers at the pizza place. Maybe she could just make sure he's okay and then never speak to him again. Or maybe she was supposed to meet him and save him from entering dark alley ways in the city after midnight like a complete idiot and that's it. Done.

hows your head she texts back against her better judgement.

fine she gets in response. Jaeli barely has time to read it before her phone is dinging again. **should I take this sudden interest as a sign ive won you over w my knightly defeat of that terrifying robber last night**

she was a little grl and u knocked urself out while letting her get away

that wasnt a no ;-)

Yeah, Jaeli felt nothing for that wink. **this is. NO.**

He sends a broken heart back and Jaeli goes on with her day. She wouldn't think about how her sisters never call, not even to reprimand her for her chat with their mom earlier, she'll just let herself get ahead on her syllabi just in case something else comes up in the future, or better yet, to prevent another 3am paper disaster.

***

The texts don't stop. It's like she has pushed some magic button that opened Oliver up and she can't find the one to shut him down again. Either that or she really is his only friend. She doesn't even have to respond for him to just keep talking. Mostly about himself. About home and how the water there is colder but looked cleaner and smelled much better and how he never thought about sharks as much without the nightly news spotting great whites off the coast of Cape Cod. How he lived above the bakery in a tiny apartment that is still bigger than his sister's in New York but somehow cheaper. About how Rose, the sister, went to school for film and worked for some popular television shows back in the UK before making contacts in the US and moving over. Her goal is Hollywood. Apparently when she was in school she used to fake an American accent and say she was a movie star just visiting Scotland to film. It didn't take her long to decide life behind the camera was more her speed.

CAUGHT IN A LIE

He talks about his art, how he wants to show in a gallery, but he never gets good feedback on work that comes from his own brain, only commissions. How he paints stories his grandmother used to tell him when he was little and he and his family thought they were the best thing but it was hard to believe it when no one else wants to even look at them.

Jaeli almost feels like she's traded her sisters for the near nonstop flood of text speak and slang that she takes too long deciphering, but she can't deny that he is interesting. A bit of fresh air mixed with her musty, second hand text books.

She feels as though she knows him, even more after a couple weeks of reading text messages and listening to brief voice mails inviting her for coffee, more than she did from the dreams. And that's probably a good thing whether she wants to know him or not. It makes him more separate, more real.

A human being.

An artist slash part time pastry decorator and waiter from Thurso with family and friends back home.

A person with more than a contagious laugh and an unfortunate knack for being in the wrong place at the wrong time, even if the real Oliver might have a little of that himself.

Trisha, Alexandra and occasionally Theo start to spend more and more time at the bakery and soon it's too hard to ignore their pleas for study dates. The first time she returns with them in those weeks apart, you would think Jaeli delivered the sun with her. Surely someone who reminded her more of an excited puppy that a self-respecting man had to be annoying, right?

It's just a little hard not being happy yourself at having someone so happy to see you, so impressed by you. She has no idea what she has done to win him over, but it is apparently something she's got going for her.

EMILY TALLMAN

"Jaeli! We were just talking about the Halloween party the undergrads are throwing at the Sigma Phi Epsilon house and thinking about maybe crashing it for a little fun. Blow off some mid-semester steam. How about it?" Alex announces with excitement as Jaeli takes her seat.

"Halloween isn't for a couple more weeks."

"And so is the party. Plenty of time to remove the stick from your butt and pick a costume." Trisha says, more to the laptop screen in front of her than to Jaeli.

"Hahaha. I'll think about it. Are you going Lucky Charms?" Jaeli askes in Oliver's general direction.

It takes him a minute before he does a double take her way. "Excuse me! Was tha meant for me? Lucky Charms? I'm appalled. Offended. How dare you? I've told you again and again I'm Scottish. I'm no leprechaun. I can't believe you've done this. You're breakin' me heart!"

"I know, I just wanted to see that stupid grin slide off your face."

"You're so charming. Ya know tha? I don't know why I even put up with it. An' here I was goin' to go invite you to mi art show. But fine, I know where I'm not wanted." The stupid grin is slowly making its way back on his face. It's a shame, he could have a gift with sarcasm if not for the horrible poker face.

"Shut up and tell me when it is."

"You're real hard tae please, ya know tha?"

"We tell her all the time." Trisha mumbles, holding out a hand for the cupcake Oliver is bringing her way.

"Well maybe if I was plied with baked goods—" The cupcake immediately changes directions and Trisha has to break the mind meld she's forming with her Mac book to jump up and snatch it back.

"Ya dinnae even look at the flower I put on it. You were supposed tae give me an opinion on if it was girly yet sophisticated

CAUGHT IN A LIE

enough for the bleeding bridal shower ya git." Oliver screeches at Trish as she plugs back into the matrix and finishes devouring the treat.

Jaeli is trying to convince herself that maybe she has more of a crush than she seriously didn't even think about, and that maybe she's the tiniest amount possible jealous of her friend's interactions with Oliver. Of their comfort at just letting him invade their little group but Jaeli has a feeling it was more of that same, cornered, threatening fear from the other night raising its ugly head. She couldn't control him, he's a person not a pet or a story. And she can't ask her friends not to spend time with him, it's way too late for that. So let the internal freak out commence. The fact is that Oliver is an interesting guy, someone who shows interest in her whether she wants it or not, and she can't do anything about it. It's frustrating. And nerve-wracking. She isn't going to survive this. She must have a look on her face. A look saying she's debating how she could stop being friends with these people to avoid them hating her in a time when she doesn't even have her family because of the same mistake, because Alex is giving her worried eyes and not so subtly nudging Trisha out of her tech stupor. "It's nothing." Jaeli says, cutting off the question at its throat. But Alex seems to get it. Or at least that it's about Oliver if the cold shoulder she gives him for the rest of the study group is any indication.

At first she's impressed by how easy it was to get Alex back on her side, firmly planted in the 'we don't like this Oliver' circle, but then she catches her friend trying not to laugh a couple times and feels a pang of guilt. The kicker is an innocent **did I do something unamerican to alex? how do I fix it** from Oliver. It hits her again, how incredibly selfish she must be.

She catches Alex's eyes, looks pointedly at the moping Oliver now avoiding them behind the counter and mouths *it's fine.* The spell is suddenly broken and Jaeli wants to kick herself. She needs to choose. Tell or don't. She needs a firm decision to measure her future choices and social interaction by or she is going to need to leave all of this behind and she really doesn't want to do that.

A twinging headache forms behind her right eyebrow as she sets her resolve.

She needs to keep lying.

CHAPTER NINE

*J*aeli's preschool class is abuzz the day of her teacher's gender reveal party. All the boy's placemats are decorated blue and all the girl's are pink. They have a vote and two big balloons in the front of the room are filled with confetti, ready to be popped after Mrs. Jen lets them know if the little black and white picture of a cloud looking thing in the front of the room is a boy or a girl. They've just had pizza strips and fruit cups and they're finishing up a story when her classmates start to ask questions. Jaeli has a question to. She squirms in her seat, hand stretched up as far as she can reach. She's been sad all day. So sad so many people were happy about something that her teacher was so sad about. When she is finally picked Jaeli's little voice asks "Why are we naming a dead thing?"

Her teacher looks shocked but she should know, Jaeli has seen her so sad and crying and even not coming back to school. "Jaeli, what do you mean honey? This little baby is a miracle. We just heard its heart beat yesterday at the doctor. There's nothing *wrong. In just 3 months you'll get to see. I'll do a special show and tell." Jaeli knows it's not true. She's mad that Mrs. Jen would lie. She hates it when people lie to her. Only bad people lie. "Alright everyone! Who is ready to pop a balloon?"*

The room cheers and Jaeli's question is forgotten until her mom comes to pick her up and stays after school with Mrs Jen for a very long time.

Two weeks later, Miss Potter is their new teacher for the rest of the year. Mrs. Jen never brings the baby boy to show and tell.

***

A dozen more "*I'm fine*"s to the point where she is actually starting to believe it and Jaeli finds herself trying to parallel park to the very unhelpful beat of Trisha's passenger panic breaking outside a pretty swanky looking restaurant a block over from where Oliver's art thing is supposed to be. They're going to be a little late, city parking when you don't trust your debit card enough to cover a parking garage fee is a little daunting. Her tire bumps up against the curb in reverse and again when she tries to straighten forward so she calls it quits. "Come on, let's go pretend we know the difference between expressionism and impressionism."

"Oh hun, at least you know enough to make a joke? You can just pretend you're a hipster with Theo and Alex."

"Hopefully. When did they say they were getting here?"

"Um... Is here the building that's in darkness? I knew we were late but I thought it was fashionably, not this late."

"See. Told you I had a sixth sense about parking. We would have paid 18 bucks for nothing." Jaeli pulls out her phone to text Oliver and make sure they have the right address when he steps off the darkened stoop.

"Hello Ladies. Lovely evening."

"You didn't lure us to a dark abandoned building to kill us did you?" Trisha stops mid step, leaning back, completely ready to bolt for the car, hopefully in a teasing way.

"Erm, no?"

"Okay... work with me here, does you stuff glow in the dark?"

"Do you see a glow Trish?"

"What happened?" Jaeli asks, sensing a brewing breakdown in 3,2,1...

"Well, it would appear the right arseholes that own this resplendent little space cared not to mention that they couldn't make this month's rent. Or last months for that matter. They certainly didn't see anything wrong with charging me what I thought at the time was an outrageous amount to show my work here tonight, or ya know, even give me a head's up last night when I was dropping off my work that they wouldn't be opening today. What do I even do? I've called them a dozen times but they donnae answer. I've had to turn people away. Actual people with nice coats and purses I might've guilted into buying something. Christ. I can't even get my work." He presses his face against the wall of reinforced windows. "I can see it all right there, they didn't even hang anything. I can't believe this."

Alex and Theo come around the opposite corner, Theo seeing Oliver stepping away from the windows and already raising his hands in greeting. Jaeli tries to shake her head but it's too late. "Hey! Big man! How's the show going, are you rich yet?"

"Congratulations, we're so excited to see everything! We want to pick something for the apartment or at least ask for a commission in front of some snobs. What do you think?"

"I think I need to get blutered, any one up for a swally?"

Theo's eyes looked like they were trying to escape his head. At least she isn't the only one that felt like this half the time Oliver opened his mouth. "I'm sorry. You want a blue turd?"

80

"What? Blutered." Oliver repeats, Theo shakes his head while all three girls smile down at the sidewalk. Jaeli's shoulders are not at all starting to shake. "Blutered, ya ken? Guttered? Pissed? Hammered? Plastered, come on!"

"Oh, drunk?" Theo guesses, proud of himself.

"Yes! God."

"Good, for a minute there I thought you were talking about something kinky."

"Well, I wouldn't mind a bit o' that either." He actually has the gall to wink at Jaeli. She is not impressed.

"So what happened?" Alex askes before Jaeli could start an angry rant at the poor guy who was just joking after a horrible day.

"You find out, you tell me. I just want my paintings back. I've got a sculpture in there too, not for sale, it's just important. I'm at the point where I almost don't even care about the money. I just want me work back. Can you call the cops on something like this?"

As four grad students and a foreigner, they were starting to realize they had a pretty small amount of life experience when it came to how to handle this situation. It seems, at least for the moment, that Oliver's idea to get *blutered* wasn't necessarily a bad one. It's a Friday, they have nowhere to be and a lot of individual steam to blow off apparently. Alex vented about not being particularly fond of Trisha's aunt and Theo's mom or the pressure she was putting on their relationship. Theo's stage manager is micromanaging everything to the point where her own work wasn't getting done and Theo has been having to pick that up too. Trisha's mind circled around money woes and her unraveling thesis idea, some of which Oliver was actually able to help with. Oliver's night was self-explanatory, though he did begin to harp on his luck and a bit of self-consciousness she had never really seen in him. Apparently no one was a fan of his art. How it was too dark and he should be thankful it wouldn't be in the paper tomorrow to ruin what little hopes he had left.

CAUGHT IN A LIE

Jaeli doesn't say anything about herself. Just observes and catalogs. DreamOliver had seemed so strong and confident. So sure of himself. It's interesting to find the little flaws in this Oliver, the things that make him different and real. The bitchfest continues into the night until Trisha realizes that Jaeli still hasn't contributed anything other than pats on the back and hopeful words.

"You take the cake honey, your life is so ridiculously fucked right now." Trisha says, slopping a little of her drink as she gestures towards Jaeli. "Get it out. Come on. I know you're dyin' to."

Jaeli stares at her for a second, feeling Oliver give her a look that itches her skin. That familiar cornered, threatened fear freezes her spine a bit straighter.

"Trisha, I think it's time you're cut off now." Theo steps in, a worried look in his eyes Jaeli is going to ignore. She doesn't deserve that look. Sure she has things to share but she *can't* share them and that is no one's fault but her own.

"Are you ok lass?" Oliver leans over to ask, brogue thick with drink and probably some residual anger. They have been asking him to slow down and repeat or reword all night, his accent apparently getting thicker the more emotional he gets.

"Yeah. Fine. Just some family stuff. Nothing to worry about." Jaeli spits out quickly, hoping it's close enough to the truth that it doesn't count as another lie.

"Liar!" Trisha shouts and points at her. The accusation makes her jump and blush, the soda rolling in her stomach. She feels sick.

"I think I need to leave. Trisha, do you need a ride?" Jaeli needs out of this situation. She is going to throw up or worse, word vomit, but she can't leave Trisha to spill the beans in her absence either. At least not in front of Oliver.

Luckily Alex handles that one, nudging Trisha off her stool and offering to walk back to the boarded-up gallery with Oliver to see if anything has changed and check for some sort of sign from the owners one more time. She tells him they could give him a ride to the police station in the morning if he doesn't hear anything by then too.

As Jaeli waves her goodbyes and tugs Trisha behind her back down the block towards the car, she prays that they stick to their word and don't let Oliver do something drunk and stupid like try to break in.

Her prayers aren't answered. At first she thinks the call at one AM when she's just pulling on nice comfy pajamas after the horrible tight dress and suffocating nylons she had worn to the not-art-show is one of her sisters caving, but no. It's Alex, calling from the police station. Luckily, the owners are not pressing any kind of charges and even luckier, the silent alarm got the building owner's attention and Oliver is going to be able to legally pick up his art at ten AM tomorrow. He's also getting his rental fee back. Unluckily, they did get a wagon ride to the station and need to be picked up if possible. Jaeli slides her bare feet into her most comfortable Converse and gives her bed a wistful look before heading out the door again.

CHAPTER TEN

Midterms make it easy to avoid another group confrontation until Halloween. It seems that everyone is still on the frat Halloween party train and they inevitably convince Jaeli to come along. She secretly loves Halloween. More so when she's home and can celebrate with her family. It's the sexy costumes and drunk undergrads that have her rolling her eyes and dragging her heels. She tries to snap discreet pictures on her phone of the various "gypsies" or "Esmeraldas" she sees, thinking of Catherine and how offended she'd be or her mother and how she would be trying to cover everyone up or give them tips on traditional Romani dress for next year.

Alex and Theo look pretty spectacular in their punk rock outfits. She doesn't think Alex had to dig too deep into her wardrobe to put the look together, but Theo is probably dying on the inside a little. He looks so cold without his flannel. And he's wearing contacts, that's love right there. She says as much to Trisha and sends her friend cackling over to share the thought, kitty tail swinging in her wake.

Jaeli tugs at her own cat ears, itching underneath the too tight headband. It was this or nothing, Jaeli was very happy with nothing but according to Trisha the dollar bin at Walgreens was a must before heading back to campus. At least she was already wearing all black and it matched.

A loud *boo!* from behind her paired with a little shove has her screeching. It isn't her finest moment, this is exactly why she didn't want to come. Parties were for the end of the semester when all the stress was behind you, not when you were still a wound up ball of *waiting for test scores* and *oh God there's still half a semester left*. Her friends turn to her just in time to see Oliver circle around making what is probably supposed to be ghostly fingers at her.

He is covered in black and white make up, impressively done. He almost looks like he has stepped out of a silent film. Of course, his laughter booming at her kind of ruins the effect. Trisha and Alex take in the sight with expressions carefully blank, waiting on Jaeli's reaction before deciding what to do.

"Aw, come on guys." Oliver hoots. "I'm the ghost of Oliver Scott. I've come to haunt you Jaeli! Oooo." He says, pitching his voice up and down, obviously having a lot of fun.

Shit.

No one is laughing. Jaeli is sure her pallor is probably beginning to match his. She lets out a nervous chuckle for his benefit but he obviously sees right through it, giving her an expression that is not at all impressed. "You guys are ridiculous. This costume is great. I don't think I'm ever going to get American humor. I should have listened to Rose and been a zombie." He gestured at one shambling by them.

"I was just surprised. You really do look great. How did you do all that make up by yourself?" Jaeli asks, trying to get conversation going again and away from the painfully obvious reason she and everyone else is uncomfortable, less someone say something. It is a curse. All the best Romani curses are on one's self. Would every time they get together be like this?

"Now you're just trying to flatter me. I won't fall for it." He beams at her.

"Suuure." Theo drags out, rolling his eyes at how easy it is to please their new friend. Oliver talks about his process and complements Alex and Theo, flirting playfully and making more slang jokes at Trisha they all were learning to just roll with.

Jaeli takes the opportunity to take him in. His eyes dance between them all as he speaks, his hands are gesturing wildly and he's very much enjoying the free booze moving loose and comfortably in the crowd. Those eyes never stop dragging her in, though. Even when she's uncomfortable or angry, they catch her. Especially now being the only specks of color on him, making them really stand out. They are stunning. A kind of blue she has never seen in real life before, surprising in this light. They were usually so dark, but now against his powder white face, they are lit up with his laughter, glowing and showing off the sparks of lighter tones within them. It's nice to see Oliver having such a good time after the failed art show.

She doesn't realize the conversation has slowed to a stop until his eyes are locked on hers and a slow smile is spreading across his mouth. She has seen that smile before and would bet her last dime that his makeup is covering a splotchy blush. She clears her throat and looks down into her drink, guessing how much longer she could sip at it until she'll be forced to trudge through the masses to get another. "Can I grab you a fresh one?" Oliver asks, reading her mind. She smiles up at him and shakes her head a little, looking over his shoulder to a glaring Alex. She looks worried, maybe even angry and all that squinted eyed focus is baring right into the back of Oliver's head. It was a wonder he wasn't bursting into flames.

For all the times they have talked about the real Oliver, Alex had been blessedly silent. Unlike Trisha who is shipping them like one of Ariel's school mates, saying it must be some cruel joke from fate but fated none the less almost every time they hung out. Jaeli's starting to get the feeling that Alexandra feels the opposite. This couldn't be good.

Jaeli is proven right when Oliver finally books another, albeit smaller and all around less impressive, gallery. Jaeli is surprised at the number of people who were willing to walk up seven floors to the suffocating small loft with odd lighting and their own soft music being overpowered by what sounded like a one man show on the floor above. Apparently the venue is the hipster thing to do when you showcased in Oliver's genre. The night is going well, if a bit stuffy. She doesn't fully understand what the people around her are talking about but knows she is in immediate awe of Oliver's work. It's very different from the small portfolio of commission pictures he'd shown them almost two months ago.

Theo returns with two glasses of wine, one for himself and one for Jaeli, Alex right beside him. Trisha couldn't join them tonight, work obligations she had said but Jaeli knew she was hiding a date with a girl she met in PoliSci that she isn't ready to tell the others about yet. They silently analyze the painting in front of them, Jaeli's eyes raking over the colors and folds of fabric in the wind. She can almost feel the life there, hear the sound of it. How has Oliver's work not become more popular? Did he show it enough? Maybe that hint of self-consciousness she has been seeing more and more of lately is crippling him, he has to just be assuming people don't like or understand it. She turns to Alex, mouth already gasping in air to fuel her wonder when she takes in her friend's expression.

Alex has that disapproving squint on again. Theo is almost mirroring it, eyes locked on the figure just off center.

"What?" Jaeli asks, turning back to the painting and looking for an extra arm somewhere or something horrible that she'd missed.

Alex lets out a quick sigh and a couple verbal pauses before shrugging and turning to face Jaeli. "It's just so… depressing. It's

CAUGHT IN A LIE

like looking at an image of *no hope*. Like watching someone hit rock bottom and not get up. You don't think Olli is, maybe, depressed?... Do you?"

"No." Jaeli said quickly, looking back at the painting in question. It's an act of suicide at first glance, but it's so much more than that. It's not a portrait of *no hope* as Alex had said, it' a depiction of immediate regret in the moment of that last step. It's a lesson. If anything, it's absolute hope! Sure it's dark, but it's full of light too, and besides, "They're all based on stories."

"Hmm?"

"Seriously. He told us a few times. They're stories his grandmother told him." The skeptical look isn't moving off her friend's face. "*What*?"

"Nothing. I'm just a little worried I guess."

"I told you, they're just his grandma's old stories. He does plenty of other lively commissions full of rainbows and glitter and whatever people ask for. You've seen them. One was of pink kittens in a friggin meadow. Come on."

"I don't know. It's just odd, isn't it?"

"What is? The painting? I don't know. These hooded things must show up in the stories a lot. Maybe it's a Scottish thing we're not getting."

"No, Jaeli. Meeting two people with the same name, from the same far away country, with the same looks? The same meet up story—"

"Technically we met the day before!" Jaeli cuts in, sweat starting to bead at her temples and run its slimy fingers down her spine. God, she could almost swear she could smell herself but she is just as sure it's the creaky, old building around them.

"I'd say you were lying if the coincidence of a real life Oliver wasn't so absolutely impossible! Like is this guy—"

"*Alex.*" Theo snapped, not doing much good, but Jaeli is thankful for the slight pause none the less.

"No. I'm gunna say it. It's weird that your ex has a doppelganger. Ok? Are you sure you like him for the right reasons and not just because of the similarities? Are you positive this isn't some long con? I'm worried alright. I'm allowed to be. I'm your friend and I don't want to see you get hurt like that again."

Jaeli doesn't deserve friends, never mind friends as caring as this. Good people who trust her. They deserve someone she can't be, someone honest and whole and not sweating like a pig at the thought of them hating her even for a second. "Would it make you feel better if I said I was psychic and dreamt up the other Oliver and this one is the real deal?" She can at least try, right? Try giving them something honest, even if it is just testing the waters and another trick.

"No. I'd feel like I was on Beyond Belief." Alex snaps, hand making angry cutting motions that have Jaeli stepping back.

"Ugh, I thought I banned you from ChillerTV." Theo mumbles, giving Jaeli a 'what can you do' shrug. She owes him.

"And I thought I said no Doritos while touching my new controllers. Seriously though. You're a psych major Jae. You guys don't believe in that stuff. I'm finding it a lot easier to believe the whole evil twin thing."

"Psych major and also Rom." Jaeli deadpans. That line between being secretive and coming clean is getting pretty thin tonight. She has to be out of her mind, she just can't take it anymore. Alex rolls her eyes and Jaeli's stomach clenches to the point where she's not even sure if she's breathing anymore. She takes in a deep breath, letting it out as an exasperated sigh, she is so close and yet she still can't do it. "I'm just trying to say don't worry about it. I'm erring on the side of caution and besides, we're just friends. Nothing is going to come of this."

"Mhmm" Alex and Theo hum at the same time, tilting their heads in sync at the next painting. That was far creepier than whatever Alex was shivering over in the next frame.

CAUGHT IN A LIE

Jaeli scoots over to take a peek, it gives her chills too, but she is thinking it's for different reasons. Hers more in the lighting and emotions aspect and Alex maybe on the hooded figure standing on the railing of the bridge, watching a procession of cars across the river. Okay, maybe the figures cloaked in darkness throughout Olli's work are a little creepy. But they're also really beautifully done.

Soon enough Oliver joins their little party with a glass of wine in each hand, frowning a little at Jaeli's full glass before passing it off to a very bored looking Theo. "Thanks for coming you guys. Sorry it's a little cramped. Having a good time, are we?"

"Great." Jaeli smiles. "Really impressive stuff here Oliver. I didn't know you sculpted." She gestures to the center of the room at a large statue, sculpture, whatever the correct term is for the massive cloaked figure under a solitary light bulb, the only light in the room besides the spot lights at each painting and around the statue's base, hanging bare from the fixture. That one is definitely a little creepy, the way the spot lights hit everything from the bottom and send shadows arching throughout the room and dancing into the grooves of fabric Oliver carved out, "How on earth did you get that thing up here?"

"It's hollow actually. Wire frame with fabric plastered over it and a barrow full of paint. You like it?"

"I honestly like the paintings better."

Oliver laughs. "Its eyes do have a way of following you under that hood, don't they? I mean, ya can't even see 'em and yet, they watch you. Yeah, Mick gives me the creepies sometimes too."

"Mick?" Alex asks, biting off the same question from Jaeli. He names the monsters?

"Aw yeah. Mick, John, that one over there's Shelly." Oliver smiles like he was laying out a punch line but never delivers it. Jaeli can't help but copy him, it's contagious. She can't help but notice the cheer back in his eyes too, the nerves he had coming over falling off of him as they speak. She snaps herself out of it with too big a sip of wine. She feels like an ass staring at someone's eyes so often when she hated that people stared at her own mismatched pair.

"So there are people under the cloaks?" Jaeli askes, studying a painting she's already seen but not wanting to look anyone in the eye at the moment.

"You could say tha' I guess." Oliver says, that same knowing smirk crooking his mouth in the corner of her vision as he steps up beside her to watch her look over the piece.

"Maybe you'll paint one of us one day." She doesn't know why she says it, just a feeling or a question. Maybe a want to have that much attention from him and that much feeling that she herself would be a person in the background of one of the paintings.

"Mm. I don't think you'd like that. They're not the happiest of pieces you ken? I wouldn't want any of you to be in a position like that." He nods to the cloaked figure kneeling down on the ground in front of a marsh, mud dripping from soaked cloth and clenched fists. He's probably right. Maybe Alex is a little right too.

Chapter Eleven

As the weeks go on, Jaeli worries. It's what she does when she knows someone has a problem and doesn't want to talk about it. She can only help people if they tell her what's wrong.

The hooded figure is back in her dreams, haunting and hunting Oliver. Stepping out of his paintings to shoot him down and leave her crying for help, too late to do anything. The dreams drag on, always her too late and holding an Oliver with no life in his eyes. It doesn't help that booming thunder has woken her up the last few nights and the days have been wet, cold and dreary.

It gets to the point where she thinks maybe she needs to talk to him. Maybe Alex is onto something. Maybe she is waiting too long to confront him and maybe he is depressed and maybe even a danger to himself.

Or maybe, and more likely Jaeli thinks when she walked into the bakery harried from rushing off campus in the rain to hear him mid booming laugh and see his beet red face full of joy and rib bursting delight at whatever joke she's missed, maybe her dreams are about her lies killing her relationships and how she is waiting too long to tell everyone. As her dreams seemed to be confirming for her, it is too late. She shakes the rain off herself, wiping her soaked hair out of her face and behind her ears as best as she can.

So she will address what small problems she can, she'll talk to Oliver and make sure he's okay before Thanksgiving comes up and everyone goes their separate ways and leaves him on his own for a long weekend or so.

"Jaeli! Please tell me you're not going to stuff yourself on pies and join the cast of peopleofblackfriday.com next week! God, have you seen this site? Theo was just showing me. Atrocious. You're far too lovely for it." He tugs a dish towel from his apron ties that is only slightly stained with frosting and offers it to her, she gladly accepts it.

"I prefer sleep to waiting in line for hours in the cold, thanks. Besides, I never have enough money for the big stuff and all the little stuff is still left by the time I roll out of bed the next day." Jaeli grins, thanking her blessings for the perfect subject. "What are your plans next week? Are you staying here or going to visit your sister?"

"Ah, no use wasting the petrol to celebrate a holiday we never have before. Besides, I've got a shift here on Thursday morning and again Friday."

"So you're going to be all alone?"

"Don't say it like that. I'm alone all the time. I'll get some paintings done and work. It'll be nothing. 'Sides, I didn't think you cared." God, how can a person make themselves look so much like a puppy and why is she so affected by it?

Jaeli's phone starts vibrating in her pocket, shocking her. She does a quick take of their usual table by the window. Alex, Trisha and Theo are all huddled around warm coffee and the glows of their laptops so that can only mean one thing, family. Jaeli panics,

CAUGHT IN A LIE

whipping back out the door and huddling under the bakery's less than waterproof awning for some privacy.

"Hello?" She shouts a bit into her phone over the sounds of rain and traffic.

"Jaejae, baby I have very bad news." Her mother coos at her, voice a little rough like she just got off a yelling phone call herself. It is very possible.

"What! What? Get it out you're scaring me!"

"Everyone is okay chav, but you cannot come home to celebrate the thanks giving with us."

Jaeli should have thought of that. Of how she hasn't spoken with any of them in over a month. How she was supposed to contact them when she is ready, and apparently she hasn't been ready yet. How that meant she has nowhere to go this holiday either. It's odd how a little weight comes off her chest at that. "I understand, mom. I shouldn't have just assumed. I was going to call, it's just been busy.

"No baby, there's been a flood. Marianna's house is gone. Everyone is okay but our house is bad too. Lots of water in the bottom. Everyone is going to stay on the top floor. We are ok, I didn't want you to see the pictures on the news and worry."

"The news?"

Jaeli marches back inside and gestures for Theo's laptop since he is just using it to laugh at Wal-Mart goers. She didn't even know that site was still a thing. She goes to their local news stations website and watches a video of their mall filling with water, of ladders from fire trucks reaching across lake like streets to get people from top floors of duplexes and even her sister's house, floating pink playhouse from when Ariel was little and all, completely engulfed by water. She gasps at the missing people reports and has to remind herself that her mother is on the phone, her family is okay.

"Mama. Mari and Ariel, they're there with you? Oh my God."

"Yes honey. Catherine too and Jason and that stupid cat. Scott is still in Florida and he's going to stay there with his friends. We're ok. But no big holiday ok? I leave you alone again now, just don't worry. Love you Jaejae."

"Mom, wait!" Her mother doesn't say anything but she doesn't hang up either. "Maybe you guys can come up to me. I'll clean the apartment. Maybe I can show you some nice places to shop. We could all pitch in on dinner. I think I can squeeze you all in to sleep over too. You shouldn't sleep in a house that still has water in it, especially since the storm isn't over. Please mom. Can you get here?"

"If you think we can fit then we will come. Do you think it's ok if we maybe come tomorrow morning? It's too late today and Jason is very angry I don't want him to drive us in the rain. My little van can only take so much. I'm surprised she didn't float away too."

"Of course mom. Whatever you need. Call me if it gets worse, promise?"

They say their goodbyes before she realizes how quickly her mother agreed. Jaeli has the distinct feeling she's just fallen into a trap, but she can't find it in herself to care, she's just thanking the stars that her family is okay.

"Hey." Trisha says, reaching across the table to touch the hand Jaeli still has clasped tight around her phone. They are all huddled around the pictures and videos on the website Jaeli had brought up. "Everything okay?"

"I think so." Jaeli whispers, falling into a seat Oliver has pulled up for her.

"I heard ya. I didn't mean tae, but I did and if you need anythin'. I have room upstairs, I can help. Whatever you need Jaeli." Oliver says, kneeling down next to her.

"It's not that bad. Everyone's ok. They had my mom's house to go to so I think they're going to be fine. It's just stuff that's gone. Stuff is nothing. I thought when she first called that it was people."

CAUGHT IN A LIE

"You love are either in shock or extremely well adjusted." Oliver jokes, tapping a knuckle under her chin in a way that would have her glaring if it had been anyone else. "How about a cuppa and a nice fired roll, eh?"

They sit in silence for a little while, watching the flood pictures flit slideshow style over the screen. "Does anybody know how to cook a turkey?" Jaeli askes, at least it has her friends looking at her with smiles again.

"Aye. I think I can help you with that."

"How would you like to have your first ever Thanksgiving in an overcrowded apartment full of cranky flood victims?"

"Well when you put it like tha'." He winks at her. "Sounds like a party." He squeezes her shoulder as he leans over to put her tea on the table in front of her. This is probably a mistake, but if she doesn't have to wash a giant smelly bird and her family still got fed, she couldn't care less. Besides, at least her family would be a group of people who knew her secret. Even if Oliver still didn't, maybe it could be a day where she didn't have to feel the need to control every subject that came up.

The only problem is that her family doesn't actually know. And of course Jaeli doesn't find out until the last minute.

"*Mom!* How could you not tell them?"

"How could I? It was your secret, I would not tell that. What you must think of me!"

CHAPTER TWELVE

As the fates would have it, her mother decides it would be best to stay in Rhode Island until Thanksgiving Day. "To get things settled" she put it. That's fine with Jaeli. Once she gets home, she realizes her apartment is much smaller than she had thought. Living by herself, especially these last phone call less months, her space felt so huge and lonely.

Well, apparently her living room was so small that her pull out couch wasn't exactly pull-out-able and then space in her bedroom in no way supported the blow up mattress as she thought it would. The only thing she could think to do is move her couch sideways and open it into the little kitchen area, but then there was the matter of the table which she can't move out until Thanksgiving dinner and there really isn't anywhere to store it anyway. She's mid panic when her mother called to reschedule. It's one hell of a breath of fresh air.

Later she will figure out Jason could sleep on the couch, Marianna and Ariel on the blow up mattress on the floor of the living

CAUGHT IN A LIE

room and her mother in her bed with her. Or some variation there of once they all arrive and argue locations. She'll try not to worry about it until Wednesday night when she's setting things up.

And washing a hideously smelly turkey.

"It was never like this when we picked up a bird from the butcher at Christmas." Oliver brushes off, not wanting to wash the thing either. Must be nice having someone wash a slimy, foul smelling, frankly disgusting carcass of a thing for you. Jaeli remembers her mother doing this frequently, but she never realized it was so bloody, and the texture... Jaeli never needed to know what a heart, liver, or kidneys felt like. To think her mom used to wash and cook those as well and put them outside for the neighborhood strays. No thank you, in the trash they go along with an entire roll of dirty paper towels. The smell starts to overtake her again, it must be the metal sink. She thinks the stuffing will be made of her own vomit this year before Oliver mans up and pushes her out of the way looking just as lost in what to do but thankfully less bothered by the odor. She has no idea how her mother does something like this for them so often and all of a sudden this ache hits her. She misses her family so much. She's almost not even dreading the drama that's sure to ensue or the stress of having Oliver there to witness it. She just wants her mom.

Jaeli was just as lost with the turkey when it came to the roasting part. She has her mother's stuffing recipe which was an unfortunate measuring disaster, something she's had to rework twice before opting to stuff the bird with apples and oranges like it was Christmas and starting a fresh batch just to bake by itself and serve as a side. It isn't her fault. The recipe literally calls for "one of your grandmother's tall glasses of milk and your father's brandy glass of melted butter. Enough mushrooms per slice of bread". Etcetera. There is no actual amount of bread. Mostly measurements like "enough cinnamon to color the apples, enough apples to cover the bottom of Uncle Emerest's pan." and the lovely notation of don't forget celery, onion and poultry seasoning. It's a disaster. If it wasn't so delicious, Jaeli would have called it quits and tuned into the cooking network a *long* time ago. She's just figuring out that "enough" bread is two slices per pound of turkey. She's getting the gist from there, trying to keep the balance of not too wet, not too dry with more ingredients from the list as needed.

Oliver was humming an unfamiliar but lovely tune while making a pie he insisted is the most American one he could find. It looked like apple. She's fairly certain Catherine is bringing pumpkin pie but it will be good to have variety. She's content working alongside him. They both fall into a clean as you go routine in the small space and keep to themselves. It's surprisingly comfortable. She keeps letting herself sneak little glances his way, watching him decipher the recipe and making sure everything is just right. Jaeli smiles to herself as he tries to put the crust into a glass pie plate, inevitably pulling a hole in it and swearing quietly. When he's ready to bake the bulging monstrosity she hears an ominous click click clicking from the oven and a confused "Erm…"

She steps over to see what the problem is and sees Oliver holding the faded old temperature dial in his hand. Well, that's not good.

"Please tell me you have a functioning oven." Oliver says in his best slow, clear, and patient tone.

"The stove part works and I'm pretty sure I've heated cookies up in it before." Jaeli shrugs. She's not home a lot, so sue her. She honestly didn't know there was anything wrong with the old beast.

"Okay, it bakes cookies, we can try again." He starts fiddling with the dial, trying to get it back on but every time he tries to turn it on, it would just give up on him.

Jaeli bites her lip and raises her hands in an innocent surrender. "I've honestly never tried to heat it past the first click?" She asks more than says. *Honestly.* Why was it so easy to be honest with him but no one else?

CAUGHT IN A LIE

"How have ya never used yer oven?" He is definitely judging her and it's breaking the little spell she was under just a moment ago.

"There's this thing called a college meal plan. And I have a perfectly functioning stove top, microwave and toaster." Two pieces of toast for the stuffing pop up, not quite toasted but well enough that one more round on the highest setting would be fine. Yeah, she has crap. But what else is an off campus apartment supposed to have? Half of it came from pawn shops or thrift stores, they don't exactly let you test or exchange the merchandise. The other half was already there when she moved in.

"Well what are we goin' ta do? You cake back a pie in a pot! Oh Christ, wha are we goin' to do with the damn turkey I just gave a bloody bath?"

"Do you have an oven?"

"No!" Jaeli gives him a raised eyebrow, judging him for judging her. "Thas different. I live above a bakery."

"Do you think we could use those ovens? Maybe? Pretty please?" Jaeli bats her eyelashes and sees the very second he breaks. She would have feelt bad if he lost the alpha man grump he has going on.

"This bird is the biggest pain in me arse. Are ya sure your pilgrims didn't just eat ramen? Or maybe just popcorn and your toast like Charlie Brown?"

"You've seen Charlie Brown?"

"Yes I've seen bleeding Charlie Brown. He's been on every damn day this week. An' it's cute. The smart one with the blanket reminds me o' you a bit."

"Oh yeah?"

"Aye. And unfortunately I'm the little blonde chasin' after ya." Jaeli barely got to tilt her head before he steamrolls right over that little comment. "Now, have you got anythin' I can carry this

100

home in? Because I don't care to wash it again." Oliver said, gesturing angrily at the turkey.

"I can give you a ride if you wait until I'm done with the stuffing." That seems to cheer him up at least a little. Enough for him to chatter her ear off as she works now that he isn't distracted with his own task. She tries giving him part of the recipe to sauté but it seems to be not complex enough to keep his attention.

When things are finally ready to pack up and transport Oliver gets very excited, to the point where Jaeli is worried 'give you a ride' might have somehow gotten lost in translation. When they get to the parking garage, she finally gets to relax a little as the chatter continues. "I can't believe you never said you had a car. Which one is it? I am so tired of that damned train and the taxis in this city aren't as frequent as the movies have you believe. That an' they're terrifying. Where is it?"

Jaeli just smiles and shakes her head, finally stopping at the little rust bucket she calls her own and balancing the aluminum pan of stuffing against it as she unlocked her door and the one in the back so they can put things down. Oliver goes silent as he sets down the turkey and leans back out for the stuffing and pie. The door groans as Jaeli shuts it, she leans over the console to unlock the passenger's side and nods to Oliver to get in. He pauses but gets in and buckles up none the less, mouth opening and closing like a fish for a moment while Jaeli starts it up and fiddles with the heat.

"So. This is your car then." Oliver finally says as she starts to pull out of the garage.

"Yes. I paid for it myself and everything." Jaeli says, trying to hint that he is not allowed to make fun of it. Especially if he didn't have his own.

"Oh. Thas nice." He nods, picking at a tear in the seat before catching himself and wiping his hands on his pants. "Just not what I was expecting I guess."

"What do you want, a Camero?" Jaeli definitely would.

"No, but maybe something all one color." She can feel that smirk as she sees him gesture to his door, the red one on her mostly blue car.

"It adds character." She grumbles, ignoring his amused hum.

After fumbling their heavy loads into the bakery that Oliver thankfully has the key to, Jaeli offers her services in the baking portion of the evening or to come back in the morning and help but she's brushed off with a quick but friendly, "Just put together what you want and tell me what to do." She writes down her instructions for the turkey and stuffing and helps him decipher his pie instructions.

When she's done she checks her phone to see that it's almost midnight and heads home to prepare to be invaded in the morning.

Said invasion begins at one in the afternoon, surprisingly enough. She expected them around nine or ten, but they were actually right on time. Oliver however is not. She calls and texts, only to be answered with a yelling text of **ITS NOT DONE YET**.

So dinner gets pushed back to three while they wait and watch the Macy's parade on TV and catch up. It's very quickly that Jaeli discovers her mother still hasn't told anyone her little secret and that anxiety piles on top of the fact that he still isn't there and her mother's cornbread has been devoured. They have a little round of bickering about Jaeli not telling her family herself and how silly it is to invite him even if they knew, which he still doesn't, in her bedroom away from nosy ears. She is stupid and silly and whatever slang word Oliver wants to throw at her. She just feels bad for him, being alone and painting dark things. She doesn't think he's depressed, but what if he is really good at being high functioning and just needs someone he trusted to open up to. She could be that for him. But not if her family jumps down his throat because he's the first boy she's ever brought home and they all think Jaeli has been close to dating him for almost a year! This is going to be a disaster.

Another twenty minutes of pure sweating fear pass as Ariel chatters next to her about some new show or maybe an old one as Jaeli thinks of some possible way she could cancel. Her biggest problem being that she doesn't want to lie anymore. Especially not to Oliver for some reason.

Jason looks about ready to break out the veggies her sister brought when she gets the text that Oliver is ready. She excuses herself and rushes to the café. At least the traffic from the morning had died down, everyone probably snuggled up watching the game at home after having enjoyed their feasts.

They load the car, Oliver insisting on running upstairs to change his shirt after seeing the pants and button up Jaeli is wearing. Oliver had been in sweats and a Patriots jersey, one she has never seen and she thinks maybe he had been watching American tv again and thought this is what he was supposed to wear. She'll never admit how cute that is, but he really doesn't need to change. Everyone is going to throw on sweats when they're done eating. She's pretty sure Ariel is already in leggings and what's the difference?

When they finally make it back to her apartment, Jaeli prepares him for how boring it's going to be and makes sure he actually wants to come. She probably should have done that back at his place but she's panicking a little.

"Are you okay?"

"Yeah, fine. Just, are you sure you want to subject yourself to this?"

"…yes?" Oliver asks, looking right into her eyes, his a little wide like maybe she's scaring him. Good, he should be scared. This is going to be a disaster. He's probably never going to talk to her again and that thought just feels really, really wrong. Maybe even worse than Alex and Trisha finding out. That should be weird, right?

She leads the march back upstairs and into her very loud apartment, giving him one last look and taking a deep breath before opening the door. "Um, everyone meet Oliver. Oliver, this is my mom Ana, My sister Marianna and her daughter Ariel and husband Jason and this is my sister Catherine. Okay, who's hungry?" Jaeli rushes, lifting the foil pan of stuffing with Oliver's pie stacked on top and giving them a little shake and a big smile.

She looks over at Oliver, heaving his own foil wrapped turkey pan and a shaky smile. He's nervous, red blush splotching up his face and hands crinkling the foil he's clutching.

She could do this, for him.

Maybe.

Hopefully.

Chapter Thirteen

"A Scot named Scott, huh?" Jason askes, giving Oliver a glare similar to the one Marianna was sporting over his mashed potatoes. Great, the vetting is starting, exactly what the churning lava pit in her stomach needs.

"Aye. I was going for sexy and mysterious, I see that's not taking…" Oliver jokes, pretending to eat the green beans Catherine brought. No one really likes those but it was her staple so of course when she was assigned vegetables in the potluck, this is what happened. At least mom blessed us with her mashed potatoes. Jaeli's goal was just to keep everyone from bringing desserts and missing out on turkey. She wouldn't have minded, but she had a distinct feeling the general party would have disapproved.

"More like ironic and bordering on hilarious." Marianna deadpans. She doesn't see why they're having such a problem with him if they didn't know the secret. Catherine, Ariel and her mother seem smitten enough. She also doesn't know why she cares right now. She needs to focus more on changing topics.

105

CAUGHT IN A LIE

"Funny guys are sexy here though, right?"

"Keep dreaming Glasgow." Jason rolled his eyes.

"Thurso actually."

"Excuse me?"

"Thurso, little coastal city, lots of fishing, surfing. Like a freezing cold Hawaii without all the fake luaus, just well... drunk hairy guys... maybe it's a lot more like Hawaii than I thought. Anyway, it's where I hail from. And you? Where does that tragic accent come from?" Jaeli choked a little into her cup. Oliver is doing surprisingly well handling questions from all sides, his talkative nature calming and giving everyone equal attention, sparing no one from quick little jabs once he notices the way they showed love was mostly to make fun in her family.

"You know, I've always wanted to go to Hawaii." Catherine muses, giving him a little wink. Maybe he's making certain people a little too comfortable.

"Well, that's nice I guess. Hear it's lovely."

"He's so cute Jae, good job."

Jae slaps a hand over her face "Just friends!" she yells again, it's turning into her mantra for the evening.

"Aye, so she tells me, but I don't believe her either. What do you think Mrs. Tal? Should I ask her again?" Her mother is utterly enchanted by him, nudging her under the table near constantly whenever he says something she likes or Jaeli says something she doesn't.

"Yes, yes. Did she tell you about her dreams?"

"Ma!" Jaeli gaspes. That is the exact opposite of what needs to be brought up.

"Do tell, Mrs. Tal." Oliver looks intrigued and fills his wine glass for the entertainment. An intrigued Oliver is a dangerous Oliver. This night is about to circle the drain. The lava in her stomach is about to join it, someone needs to announce volcano day, she is going to be seriously sick.

"She keeps a dream diary, you should read it. I bet there would be many interesting entries for you." She winks at him. Winked! Her mother.

"Oh my God, pass the egg nog. Someone. Please!"

"Is that right? Jae ya need tae show me this journal later."

That's it. Things are getting too close for comfort. "Over my dead body Olli." Olli, she caught herself calling him for the first time, the name tasting a little dirty in her mouth as it brings back memories of the dream him. *He* isn't *him*. Not really, but the nickname gives him such a big smile, like maybe he won something that she knew she'd find herself calling him that again. If she even gets to still speak to him after today.

"Hmm, I'm tempted but you simply look far too lovely this evening. Maybe it will be more tempting later when the holey sweats you mentioned come out? Tell me Jaelie, where are the holes exactly?"

"You think you're so cute."

"As cute as my dream self, I hope."

"More like nightmares."

Her mother claps her hands and breaks the little spell that has nearly been calming Jaeli's stomach. "Look at this passion. How can you ignore it Jaejae?"

"Jaejae! That's adorable."

Jaeli smirks, a perfect change of topic if she did say so herself. "You should hear Catherine's."

"Don't you dare!" Her sister shrieks. "Forget it was ever mentioned Oliver. Yes that's a threat. Remember who is sitting next to the carving knife." She picked up said knife and drives it into the cutting board, effectively making her point.

"My sister the Gemini, everyone." Jaeli mumbles.

"The secrets in this house." Olive marvels, "Jae, how could you think today would be boring? I think I love Thanksgiving."

CAUGHT IN A LIE

Jaeli is officially ready for some drama not involving her or family matters in anyway. She lets the awkward silence fall into distracted chewing for a minute before she sees Catherine start to fidget like she's about to say something and jumped on it. "Olli," She says, his attention immediately on her with that dopey smile again, yeah this is going to become a habit. "Did Jason tell you he loves Dollhouse?"

"Oh I knew you were a pratt the second I laid eyes on you!" Oliver throws down his napkin to gesture at her brother in law. "Sorry Ariel, for the language and the fact that your father is a blinking bawbag."

Mission complete.

The night dissolves into arguments over television, Ariel's passionate talking streaks giving Oliver's a run for their money. Dessert is eventually served when everyone has recovered from dinner and thank goodness for Catherine's pumpkin pie because Oliver's was more than a little burned and the crust was something special.

"You're a baker, how do you not know how to make pies?" Ariel asks around a polite but unenjoyable mouthful.

"No, I decorate the pastries. Sarah bakes them." Oliver says, peeling off his own crust to get to the middle which actually is pretty good.

"But Jae said—"

"That was before I really knew him." Jaeli cuts in with a smile that hopefully doesn't look too fake.

"Oh. Did you think me a dreamy baker?" Oliver smiled back. She has a feeling her dreams are never going to be let go.

"Not cute, Oliver." She mumbles again.

"He is though." Ariel deadpans.

"Thank you lass."

The noise that comes out of her niece couldn't have been human. "Oh my God, he said lass! Say it again that's even better than *aye!*" she shrieks.

Jaeli takes mercy on him and digs out the vanilla ice cream she knew Marianna had brought with her for the weekend. They end up taking apart Oliver's pie and serving a scoop of ice cream with the insides plopped on top. It's pretty great.

As they digest, conversation turns to plans for the weekend and flood damage.

"You wouldn't even believe this asshole." Marianna bitches while Oliver smirks next to her on the couch enthralled in the stories she was sprouting about her endeavors against nature. Marianna doesn't seem to be loving the attention. "He didn't even get out of the car because, and I quote, he didn't want to ruin his shoes, they're Italian. Reed Jackson, didn't vote for him the first time and never will. He's not going to help any of us. He'll probably just find a way to turn this all into profit for himself. Never trust a man with two first names Jaeli."

Jaeli laughs. "But you married one. Your son is one."

"Exactly, I'm speaking from experience."

Oliver laughs the big, deep laughs that shake his whole body and Marianna glares directly at him. It doesn't seem to faze his fun, but it's official. Her sister doesn't like him.

Soon after sunset Oliver says his goodbyes. Jaeli offers to drive him home but he says he wants to walk off dinner, he'll call her when he gets in. It's such a domestic, intimate thing *I'll call you when I get there* but Jaeli can't help but be a little relieved. She'll blame it on not having to get up and drive again. But that would be a lie, especially when that relief grows at him actually following through with a call later.

"So did you actually have a good time or were you just saying that so you could run away?" Jaeli jokes, maybe wanting to keep him on the phone a little longer, probably just getting a few minutes

CAUGHT IN A LIE

of peace from her loud and practically wedding planning family. Just friends isn't ringing through with anyone but Marianna and a still pissy Jason.

"A bit awkward but definitely worth it seeing as your ma, your sister and the little lass think I'm cute."

"You know you're cute. Shut up" Jaeli tries to make it sound as annoyed as possible.

"Such feeling right there. I can't take it, honestly."

"Shut up. I'm pretty sure Trisha has fawned on you how much of my type you are. We're just friends it doesn't matter."

"Seriously Jae, can't take all this poetry yer waxing about me right now. I'm getting all flustered. Stop."

"I'm hanging up on you." Jaeli tells him. She waits for his laugh before she does.

Her mother walks in on her holding the phone, who knows what expression on her face and that *missing you* lump in her chest beats against her heart again. Jaeli desperately craves her advice, for someone to just tell her what to do, just this once. And even though she's grown a good two feet taller than her little mama, she could really use a good hug, one of the ones that's so gentle but still tight and enveloping, that makes you feel just like a little kid again. She really fucked up, but her mom still holds her arms open to her and Jaeli wants to cry when she bends down to be held by them.

She lets her mom pet her hair for a little bit before she steps away, eyes stinging but not letting the tears fall.

"I don't know what to do mom."

"I know chav. And I can't tell you because you don't want to hear it, but the truth would not be so bad right now, yes?"

"I think it might be worse."

"Then you are not ready." They sit on the edge of her bed in silence for a while before her mother looks up at her and says the ever familiar, "Have you thought about learning the trade?"

Jaeli laughs a little to herself but thinks, what's the worst it could do? Prove one of them right? "Okay mom. Where do we start?"

CHAPTER FOURTEEN

"*He did not!*" *Jaeli throws her half empty bottle of orange soda right at Andrew's chest. He'd been talking about her father again and how her family were a bunch of homeless gypsies so watch out or Jaeli will steal your stuff! "I just saw him this weekend! Just because he doesn't live with us anymore doesn't mean he's not around. He has to travel for work. Like Matt's dad, only mine isn't sleeping with his boss!" Matt looks at Jaeli, shocked and mad, she shouldn't have known that or said anything about it, but he and his friends were being mean first. She just wants to be left alone. "My dad lives in Europe most of the year with his wife. She's a duchess. He only married her for her money, sure, but she loves him anyway and she spoils us rotten. She's pretty and kind and better than any of your step moms. I can't wait to spend the summer living in Italy and learning to sail her boat. Don't talk about what you don't know!"*

"You don't know anything loser. Your dad ran away because your mom is a bitch. He's probably working some carnival in Nebraska or something."

"Shut up! He is not! I swear, I'll put a curse on you if you don't leave me alone. You don't know anything!"

***

Jaeli talks with her mother a lot that weekend. About her dreams and not just thinking about them, but really analyzing them, remembering the little details and figuring out what they mean. They talk about weekly lessons and nightly phone calls, about meditating and learning tarot when she's ready. Jaeli agrees to come down to Rhode Island every weekend to visit and learn new things. It will be hard and time consuming, but Jaeli wants to try, even if nothing comes of it and the visits just mean she can see her mother more often. The idea is pretty cemented even before she tells her mother she has been having dreams of her choking and thought they were because they hadn't been talking, but her mother corrects her, telling her there's a tumor in her throat.

Jaeli cries, she's cut off communication with them to the point where her mother didn't tell her something so important, but apparently her mother hadn't told anyone yet.

So she goes. At first her friends think she is helping with flood recovery and she doesn't correct them. Eventually she tells them she's going home on the weekends because of family issues and to mend fences. Technically true, she tells herself. She is trying to fix things.

She's even getting calls from her sisters again. Mostly work gossip and going postal threats from Catherine and more Reed Jackson slander from Mari but there is good news mixed in sometimes and things don't seem as manic with either of them. She doesn't know if they're walking on egg shells or if things are really getting

CAUGHT IN A LIE

better, but it's nice to get the annoying interruptions again. You don't realize how much you rely on even the bad things to feel normal until they're gone.

At least she still has her friends around. Friends to borrow blow up mattresses and blankets from. And Oliver to show her how to use turkey leftovers in a pie he *could* make.

It's almost Christmas when she throws her barely constructed thesis away and starts writing on dream therapy. She thinks maybe she wants to take that route, there's an undergrad course that won't count for many credits available next semester and she is already looking up conferences she can attend. She won't be able to make it her minor or anything, not here at least, but it is something that's interesting her right now and that she has dug up a lot of material for. It's something she can be passionate about and not just word like another drool research paper. Oliver might have been right, but she'll never tell him.

She's pretty sure he already knows anyway.

Jaeli is working on said thesis, typing away on the use of dreams in modern psychotherapy when Oliver drops a dusty heavy box in front on her, the heavy thump and clink of glass possibly breaking from within effectively diverting her attention. "What is that?"

"That," Oliver points violently, "is the ridiculous box of decorations Sarah left for me to hang up. Every one of 'em were sewn wi' a hate needle an a burnin' thread. Also, we're closed, if ya didn't notice. No need to get up love, just give me the strength to decorate with such utter" He pulls something out of the box, looks at it sideways and then flings it to the side when he realizes the poor glittery mouse was once real. "Euhg. This is disgusting. God I hate this. She should have just let me go out and buy the tings. I'm gunna pull something beautiful out of mi ass, but it sure as bloody hell will be made out a shite."

EMILY TALLMAN

Jaeli laughs and started to read through what she has written as Oliver mumbles sharp criticisms under his breath at everything he pulls from the box. It feels nice, sitting in a closed bakery with him, finishing up her work and watching him fuss over a silly holiday tradition. It almost feels like home. She smiles up at him and watches him scowl at a ball of knotted ornament hooks until he feels her gaze. "What? Have I got tinsel somewhere?"

"No. I was just thinking."

"Penny for yer thoughts?"

"Are they that cheap?"

"Depends what you're thinkin' about."

"You."

Oliver's eyes dart between hers a bit flustered before he looks back into the ornament box to recover, "Well in that case, I'll give you this entire box of priceless holiday gems." He looks up at her again and must see something there in her eyes. "Jae?"

"Are you going home for Christmas?"

"Thinking about it, but I'm not sure yet. There's always Skype and I was promised unforgettable handmade manicotti if I stayed here so…"

Jaeli laughs, "You're still saying it wrong." That had been a long debate Thanksgiving Day. Her mother's half assimilated Italian-Romani mash up accent and Oliver's frustrated brogue.

Oliver doesn't end up coming for Christmas, he goes to New York to visit his sister and try to watch the ball drop. He's going to face time her if it's a success. He said his goal is to try and get a kiss from Jenny McCarthy. When Jaeli wrinkles her nose at him he tells her not to worry about that boot, he just wants to be on telly. She's happy to urban dictionary 'boot' and find it was the expected slang for ugly, she's not so happy about the judging eyebrow she's getting from Alex.

Her own Christmas is another full apartment. Her sister's house is nowhere near ready to be rebuilt, nor could they afford it right now and her mother's is on its way but still not ready to host a party.

Their holiday is without a fireplace and cramped, but it is warm and loud and smells oranges and ham, cooked thanks to Theo's oven this time. It was a further drive but well worth it when the next option was the same Chinese restaurant that yes had amazing noodles, but that she had also been eating from for the past year and a half. Manicotti is handmade on the stove top and baked at Theo's too, warm rolls toasted in a little toaster over Jaeli splurged on last time they were up here.

Presents are passed and a little table top tree decorated and all in all, it feels like one of the Christmases from her childhood. It's nice. The feeling seems to be mutual with everyone aside from Jason who keeps sneaking outside for cigarette breaks. He's wearing the coat her mother had given him last Christmas, the black pea coat with big buttons and a heavy hood. It still looks good on him, but it also still gives her that niggling little cringe in her belly. She thinks it just must remind her of Oliver's cloaked figures she'd been getting to see more of lately and tries to ignore it.

Her family stays though the New Year and her friends are invited over for her mother's annual January first lasagna, cooked in Trisha's oven this time. Maybe it is silly she doesn't have a working one. This would be the last holiday in her little off campus hovel anyway, so she doesn't mind much.

Theo and Alex can't make it, staying over the Hall's in an effort to get Mrs. Hall and Alex closer, but Trisha and Marianna became fast friends. Holiday stories from both families and new semester woes are shared along with many jokes made at Jaeli's expense. Luckily there is no talk of Oliver aside from their giggling that he didn't get his wish. He had ended up being so far away from the stage he could barely see the ball but still insists you could see his hand on tv waving frantically next to Rose's. Trisha is going to frame a screen shot with a random pair of hands circled for him and

Jaeli thinks it's a great idea, though she knows he will probably chastise them for circling the wrong pair and point out what were supposed to be his and his sisters.

Unfortunately for Oliver, the New Year comes with some bad news waiting for him outside his apartment in Boston.

***

Jaeli opened her door at ten the night Oliver is supposed to return from New York and sees a soaking wet man with his hand raised mid pounding knock and four large bags weighing down his shoulders.

"Olli." Jaeli says, not really knowing what else to say. The brief text of **I need a place to stay** had been a surprise but of course she is going to help out. She isn't expecting so many things to be with him though.

Oliver looks up at her and passes over a piece of paper. It looks like an eviction notice but that makes no sense. He lives right above where he worked, he did so much for that old bat, even grocery runs and cleaning her apartment next to his… unless he was fired too. As she kept reading, it looked like that was indeed the case.

"Olli, what happened?"

He drops his wet bags in the door way and collapses down into one of her little wooden kitchen chairs. "Well, New York was nice." He hedges. "Then, I got to meet Sarah's lovey spawn. She has apparently gone tae take up her thrown in hell and her sons are less then prizes themselves. They fired me an' I got this stapled to my door when I got home. Called them, they're gonnae sell the building. I've got two days to get everything out. I was supposed tae be out by the 30th but I told them I was out of town and at least they've been too lazy to empty out my things. So I've got the weekend before they sell everythin. My stuff too. I got all my clothes and some

CAUGHT IN A LIE

things out but my art is still there and furniture. I just have nowhere to put it. I dunno wha tae do."

Her mouth opens before she can really think about it, but she can't find herself regretting the words. "Move in with me."

"Wha?"

"Just as friends." She says slowly, making it very clear. "Until you're on your feet." Oliver nods slowly, staring at the ground, water dripping from his hair and plunking on the faded linoleum. "We just have to get you a new job." Jaeli shrugs, she doesn't know what else to offer, how to cheer him up. She has never seen him this sad, not even the night the gallery shut down with his things inside.

"About tha'" Oliver starts with a bitter laugh.

"What?"

"Well, the old job was under the table..." And Jaeli gets it, this isn't going to be easy, she doesn't even know where to start here.

"Okay, I'm not going to pretend to know the first thing about visas and living in countries other than your own, but I'm guessing confessing that little tidbit is important?"

"A bit, yeah." God, this was going to be like pulling teeth. She sits in the chair diagonal from him, giving him somewhere to look other than her if he wants and not looming over him waiting for the information. She's going to treat him like a patient for a little bit, help as best as she can and then drown him in hot chocolate and fluffy blankets until he feels better. It's an off thought for her, usually so clinical, but she's going to go with it, it feels right.

"Okay. Can you explain that to me please?"

"Well, technically I'm Rose's executive assistant, so I'm here on a work visa like her. That was going fine, because on paper she had hired someone even though she can't stand people doing things for her like tha, she's a bit of a control freak. So on paper, I'm working for her in New York and then I was going to switch over to a student visa when I applied to RISD, but I don't know if I actually

118

want to go back to school anymore and that wouldn't start until September anyway if I even managed to get in."

"So, just to be clear, you're saying you can't get a job because then it would show you weren't actually in New York with Rose?"

"Essentially yes."

"And I'm, guessing McDonalds can't be your work visa job."

"Not bloody likely." He laughs, scratching his head and looking baffled like the idea is insane for so many reasons.

"Okay, then RISD. You'll totally get in and I can help you with the applications if you want. It's better to take the risk and see what happens isn't it? Then wonder if things would have been alright and never knowing?" She's going to ignore her subconscious rolling its eyes and telling her to take her own advice sometime.

"I don't know if I'm ready to go back to school yet. I don't know if I can do it even. I wanted to try selling my art. It was a little easier in New York but..." He lets the sentence go, hanging his head again.

"But?" She tries. Oliver shrugs. "You've probably already thought of this, but what about actually going to work for Rose?"

Oliver looks at her, something in his eyes breaking her heart but she doesn't understand quite what. "I hate New York. If I have to I guess, but maybe I can try here a little longer? Just a little. I'll look inta RISD if you get sick o' me."

"That's not what I meant." Jaeli sighs. "I told you that you could stay and you can, I just don't want you to feel trapped."

Oliver hums and nods his head, falling silent. She gets the distinct feeling that he already does.

Theo, Alex and Trisha help Oliver and Jaeli move his artwork into a rented truck and then mostly into a pod they get a parking place for much to the disapproval of her landlord, even though Jaeli is allowed two spaces and two visitor spaces and the pod only takes up one. A little more than one if she is being honest, but it overlaps into her own space so she just has to be careful with her car for a little while. And, it's in a garage, it's not like it's blocking anyone's view of his dump of a complex.

Oliver's small dresser and twin bed give her a reason to put her couch back on the curb. She had expected a lot more things to be in the little apartment over the bakery, but he makes excuses that most of his belongings are still in Scotland and he had expected to be in a dorm by now. Jaeli's little living room is cramped as it is so she should be thankful. Still, it's nice to come home from a long day at school and have someone there. She thought she would hate the smell of paint, but it's actually kind of nice.

Everything is a bit nice. Better than expected at least. Much less dramatic than Alex and Theo's back and forth of half moved in at each other's places. Even though it comes with many winks from Trisha about her apartment only having one bedroom and even more hints from Alex that Theo's apartment has two. Hints Oliver is completely ignoring.

It's all going...well? It's fine, really, that strange kind of comfortable that just feels too easy most of the time.
Of course, there are little moments where the toilet paper is on the roll backwards or the cap is left off the toothpaste, that one memorable moment when Oliver left the toilet seat up and it had been too early in the morning for Jaeli to even think to look. Oh, and how he keeps writing things to pick up at the store on the magnetic message pad on the fridge. Things like that, those moments she never really believed actually happened outside TV and fight build ups in books, but there is no fight. They just keep each other company when they're free and stay in their own space when they're busy. Getting to know each other while Oliver and Jaeli are both working on their separate tasks in the bakery has been a good set up for this.

The first weekend she comes home and sees him staring blankly at a blanker canvas, paint slowly dripping down the brush

EMILY TALLMAN

and onto his hand she thinks maybe things aren't going as well as she had been assuming.

"Oliver?" She calls a couple times, inching closer. "Olli." She finally lets herself say, he lifts his head and looks a little startled that she's there. "Hey, you okay?"

"Just thinking." Jaeli nods at him, he continues to stare so she stays silent. "Donnae know what tae paint."

"Didn't you say you had a commission scheduled for this weekend? Something about tribal birds?" Jaeli had been a little distracted when he was talking on Friday, but she knows he had been excited about it. About the size of it too, that it was going to bring in some money and be something he's never really tried before.

"Mmm. Got canceled." He mumbles. Jaeli stands next to his stool and thinks with him for a bit. She can show him the tarot deck that belonged to her grandmother, one she had never seen until her mother had pulled it out of her purse this weekend. It still smelled like her father's cologne, a smell she hadn't even known she remembered. It was the one he'd wear at summer and fall Renaissance Fairs when he knew he'd sweat through his more pop culture than authentic Romani clothes by noon. Maybe Oliver could do something with the misty artwork on the cards? Maybe make a set with his cloaked figures as a quirky introduction to his art that he could sell online?

"Do you have a website?" Jaeli asks, never having thought to ask before.

"Had to make one in school but I let it go."

"Maybe we could perk it back up?"

"I don't think so. I was always horrible at it. Made my stuff look like shite because the website was so bad. I wasn't tech savvy then, now, er forget it." Oliver goes back to sighing at his canvas, wiping his hands and changing out the brush for a long pencil. Jaeli gets excited but he just continues staring, not actually making anything. At least, not that she can see, something is definitely going through his mind though.

121

CAUGHT IN A LIE

"What if I helped?"

Oliver doesn't answer so Jaeli sets her things down and fiddles with her laptop at the kitchen table. She's mostly ahead on her work, nothing due the very next day that wasn't complete at least, so she decided to fiddle with a webpage idea for a bit. It's not as easy as it looks, but at least the early days of live journal served her well when it comes to size, color, titles and links. She texts Theo a bit for some advice since he works on the webpage for his theater company, but it doesn't help much. Free websites are lackluster and difficult, websites where you could pay to have them create something for you are expensive and were looking pretty bland or very expensive and then look like they will be hard to tweak later on.

She ends up on Ariel's famed tumblr and thinks it won't be such a bad start. She flips through a few artist pages that she find and the good ones look very professional and easy to promote. She gives it a shot, entering her email, asking Oliver if he has any special name he went by when signing his art, getting back a mumbled ORS and entering it as the site name. She is a little upset that the .tumblr.com has to stay at the end, but it's only a first step and she thinks it's a pretty good one.

"Oliver, I know you're in your head right now, but do you think it would help to talk? Maybe tell me about your art. Tell me about what you paint."

"You already know."

"I know, but if I was someone seeing it for the first time, what would you want to tell me?"

"Why?"

"It's important. Just play along, okay?"

Oliver tch'd in the back of his throat and picked at the pencil in his hand. She can feel him peering at her from the corner of his eye before he starts.

"I used tae love those stories. And my mam, she hated 'em. Always tried to get gran to stop telling me 'em but I would beg her.

I don't know why. They were just great. Sad. Heartbreaking. When-ever I had a dead bad day, especially in art school when I was lonely and there was so much pressure on me to be this protégé, this artist worth the program and this man that was going to make mi family proud. To be a successful artist not some lazy bum posing as a starv-ing one – I'd think of these stories because God. It didn't matter how bad your day was, just one of these stories and you were thankful for not having such shite happen to you. Ya ken? There was always this one moment in the story that completely turned it around, and me growing up with Disney and the happy ever after deal, I'd always tink, alrioght now this is the part when they're wrong, everything really is okay. Everything is about to get better and it will all have a happy ending. But these stories never did. The people gave up. And I guess I just wanted to remind myself not to. I like these moments. I think they show the darkness of yourself, but the moment is walk-ing that edge. The person looking at this painting can look on with hope and say it will get better, they'll figure it out. Or they see the truth and know this is where things end. It's up to you. To keep be-lieving or to give up."

Jaeli types as fast and quietly as she can to keep up with what he's saying. At some point he must start drawing again. When he goes quiet and she looks up, he's hunched over a sketch pad he put up over the canvas and is moving the pencil over it with clean, smooth strokes. She gives him a little smile, not wanting to pull him out of his spell and goes back to tinkering with the website.

When she comes out of her room in the morning, she peeks into the living room to see Oliver still passed out, balled up on the little bed, the easel facing him. Jaeli can't resist taking a peek. She's stunned to see a woman staring back at her, a crooked smile on her mouth like she's about to imbue some great secret, eyes shining and hair in wild curls. Wrinkles should pull down her features, but they suit her, like maybe she has never been without them and age spots act more like beauty marks on her face. She looks equal parts tough and like she knows how to have some fun. Jaeli moves out of the way so the woman can continue to watch over Oliver as he sleeps. Later she'll take a picture of her and put it with Oliver's little blurb about his art.

She lets herself take pictures of the rest as well. The lighting in the parking garage isn't the best, but the grungy cement and corrugated metal inside the Pod accents most of the pieces in the same kind of way that the dark gallery she had first seen them in had. The ones that she thinks need more light come inside with her to have a picture taken against the brick wall in the kitchen while Oliver is sleeping. It's amazing what the man could sleep through.

CHAPTER FIFTEEN

Jaeli is having a hard time concentrating today. It's raining, the kind of cold, dark, lightning behind the clouds making them glow instead of clear strikes rain that makes her want to be at home. She would kill for a blanket and a book. One with fiction inside instead of research or theories or Dr. Bailey's dry monologues.

The rain drops streak down the textured glass of the window in little rivers that turn into blood dripping down her hand, getting stuck in the creases of her palm, darkening her life line.

"Miss Tal, do you have anything to add?" Dr. Bailey asks, "Or is the sky more interesting today?"

***

It's three weeks to spring break and her birthday when Jaeli comes home to a very paint covered Oliver and take out already on the counter. She almost falls over when she sees it's a mushroom, pepperoni and olive pie from the pizza place they found with Theo. Rizzos! The place with the perfect cheese and crust to start wars over. "What's the occasion?" Jaeli asks, hoping it's a good one.

"I got a job!"

"Really? But I thought—"

"It's another under the table job. A coffee shop. I'm a barista! This time more fancy lattes and less cake decorating, but hey, beggars cannae be choosers. Am I right? The guy said I might even get to decorate the specials board and the windows for the holidays as their last artist quit and everything's a bit out of date. I'm really going places eh?"

Jaeli gives him a smirk of her own and sits him down at the kitchen table, planting her laptop in front of him and bringing up the blog she had made for him. She had figured out how to post the pictures so no one could take them and how to tag them so they could be seen. Fandom crazy nieces were good for something. She points to his growing number of followers. "Yeah, I think you are."

Oliver seems in awe as he scrolled though the pages and reads comments. The general group of people want to know more about his work, but overall feedback is good. He quickly finds the ask box and begins answering questions. Jaeli helps him update and repost the pictures she took of each piece with a title and little blurbs. They queue up some new content and he figures out how to separate things into a group of links on the side so people can find things more easily. Next thing she knows, they're eating pizza and uploading his commissions and opening a submission box so he could potentially get more business. It's a good night and she feels happy in a way she hasn't in a long time. She is happy, yes. She's content with school and work and her friends, but tonight she feels whole. Like, yes, she is supposed to be a therapist and now she knows her concentration is going to be in dream analysis, but maybe she is supposed to be here too.

The weeks go by like that, Jaeli focusing on school, now leaving later than Oliver who has first shift at Street Corner Café. She gets home to him painting or drawing or checking his site, following and promoting the people who do the same for him. She helps answer questions for him sometimes or writes blurbs he doesn't know how to word on nights when he's busy. He helps with her things too when she's too tired. It's nice, and Jaeli's falling for the idea of this partnership a little. She can't help it.

One night, Trisha comes over with some art questions for her thesis, graduation being just a few months away. Oliver sets up a canvas and little blobs of paint for them. It feels kind of like kindergarten, but Jaeli couldn't say it isn't fun. Especially when Oliver guides her hands when she becomes frustrated with her lack of artistic skills and she leans back against him. It brings up images from the movie Ghost to her mind and she can't help thinking of all the times her mother would bring up her dreams of Oliver and how she is resisting the obvious passion between them. She knew why she resisted at first, but they have all been friends for so long now. Isn't the threat over?

While the paint is drying and Trisha is analyzing her portrait of mud, Oliver shows off his new barista skills with the new ridiculously confusing coffee machine he had gotten with his first paycheck. Trisha is happy to slurp up his work, moaning *caffeine* as she does so. Jaeli tries to refuse it but he begs her to give it a try. It does smell delicious, but she knows it will be bitter and strong and she doesn't want to make him feel bad. He goads her into one sip, but the smooth blend of flavors that hits her tongue is like no coffee she's ever tasted. She feels the heat of it go all the way down her chest as she swallows and thinks it's the most sinfully delicious thing she's ever had. She places the empty mug back on the counter at a loss for words and Oliver pushes what looks like an icing bottle of dark liquid to her. "Chocolate." He says, placing a little bag of beans next to it, "Espresso," he refills her mug and whispers,

CAUGHT IN A LIE

"magic." She looks into the mug, feeling the heat seep through her hands. "I knew you'd been drinking garbage." He preens to himself, proud to prove her wrong. It hits her as suddenly as the rush of energy through her veins, Jaeli knows she's in love. It makes her stomach hurt.

That night when they were cleaning up, Jaeli lets her hand brush over Oliver's' and finally asks him out to dinner. "I mean *dinner,* dinner. Out. With me?" She finally understands what people meant when they said butterflies would dance in their stomachs, she doesn't want to ruin the comfortable routine they've fallen into, but God does she want more. She just wants it to get even better. He doesn't disappoint her, flashing one of those bright smiles her way.

"What the hell took you so long?" He asks, bumping their foreheads together. She's almost disappointed it isn't a kiss, but his eyes so close to hers is intimate in a way that has her blushing already, burying her face in his neck and giving him a short hug before running off to bed as he calls after her.

She's such a coward but she can't help throwing the covers over herself and smiling a face aching smile where no one can see or judge. Her heart swells and she hopes this excitement never goes away.

They end up waiting just a little longer until spring break. That first week of April brings cool breezes and crocus just starting to bloom around the mulched trees lining the sidewalks on Boylston Street. They take a taxi as far as Fenway Park, the gardens, not the baseball field and walk through, taking some pictures for a faeri commission Oliver has gotten earlier in the week and some just for fun. It's nice but a little boring as they already knew each other and are two nervous idiots about what to actually do on a date. Finally Oliver puts away the camera and drags her up the street. "Come on." He would say anytime she asks where they're going. They end up in a guitar shop they had passed in the taxi. He waggles his eyebrows at her before showing off a musical talent he's been hiding on a beautiful black Epiphone he mourned to put back on the wall. When he's done with his mini concert, Jaeli drags him next door to Remy's. It's packed, the beginning of baseball season drawing fans from all over, but it's still a lot of fun to eat gourmet hot dogs and watch the game on screens the size of their living room wall.

It's not exactly the New York date from her dreams, but they do eat overpriced food "It's not overpriced if it's an experience" Oliver tells her. They buy ridiculous things, in this case the kazoos they're guilted into after playing the guitar for so long and not buying it. The Red Sox probably beat Broadway any day any way.

They stroll back over the bridge by the park, taking in the statues on their way to the mall and hotels up on Boylston. They'll be more likely to get a taxi from there without calling and waiting. They enjoying the view and quiet night when Jaeli stops them, pulling the neon yellow kazoo from Oliver's lips and replacing it with a kiss.

For a first kiss, it's terrible. Overly wet from Oliver having just been humming on the stupid toy and a bit forceful, but that was mainly from her rushing into it. Her nose shouldn't hurt after a kiss. Oliver doesn't say anything and her embarrassment and disappointment grows.

So much for passion.

She starts to walk away, but this time Oliver's hand reaches out and snags hers, stopping Jaeli and pulling her back a step. "Jae, whoa. Stop trying tae control everything, will ya love?" He huffs a laugh and leans back in, a hand tilting her face up and lips moving gently over hers. They stay that way for a moment, under the shadow of a tree next to the lapping water nearby. His nose brushes along her cheek before he leans back in and nibbled her bottom lip, pulling it into his mouth to sooth it and moving away, hand still around hers as he starts to walk again.

Much better second kiss. Perfect. Jaeli smiles and looks back up at the stars, barely peeking out from behind all the light pollution.

CAUGHT IN A LIE

"What was that thing you said? About the beautiful moonlit night back when we first met?" Oliver looks at her a bit puzzled. "When you hit your head?" The puzzlement turns to slow mortification and he covers his face with his free hand.

"Oh God, please don tell me I was singin' Sir Lauder to ya." Oliver laughs at some unknown joke. She just wants to tell him it was a lovely night. "No wonder it took you so long tae kiss me." He squeezes her hand and leans over to peck a kiss at her temple as they walk on, quiet again until Oliver steals his kazoo back and Jaeli laughs at him.

CHAPTER SIXTEEN

When Jaeli applies for graduation, she feels a bit lost. This isn't the end, she knows that. She still has her CAGS to get and maybe LMHC. She still needs to put in supervised hours before she can practice on her own. It just feels so final. Soon she'll be leaving her little ovenless apartment and... where will she go?

Jaeli has always planned on moving back to Rhode Island after she graduated, moving back home and mooching off of her mom for a while as she searched for a job and started paying back her loans. But now, with Marianna and her family there, how could she take her room back? The thing that used to be her home isn't even really livable yet. Bare floors and walls and a potential mold problem they're still looking into and her nephew coming home from Florida for the summer making things even more cramped.

The plan has been to use whatever was left of her loans to start paying off the loans and basically live until a full time job is available. But she supposes it wouldn't be too bad to put it towards

CAUGHT IN A LIE

an apartment of her own, especially since she has a roommate. She looks up from her breakfast and the final editing of her thesis and over to where Oliver is stretching in her doorway, hair rumpled and looking adorably sleepy on his day off as he shuffles over to the coffee machine.

"Hey, how would you feel about living together?" It's fun to watch Oliver's brain try and translate her meaning so early in the morning, she takes pity on him. "I mean when I graduate. In an actual apartment."

"With an oven?" She loves that his brain catches up to the places hers was going so naturally.

"Yeah. And maybe a place for your things besides the living room. It might even have two bedrooms!" Jaeli says in mock excitement.

Oliver just shrugs. "I'd like it better if we could just keep sharing the one." He winks. Jaeli hides her laughter in her corn flakes and switches tabs to Craigslist in hopes of finding something affordable.

Apartment hunting goes on the back burner for a little while as Jaeli gets swept up in finals, helping friends and family and talking with her councilors about licensing programs and job opportunities. She manages to set up more hours with CCSRI for when she gets licensed.

Soon enough she finds herself outside her Professor Sommer's office ready to slide her fifty three and a half page thesis under his door and thinking to herself how she always thinks every final paper is the worst thing she's ever written. Well, this is the last one she will ever write, hopefully, unless she went for her doctorate, and bless it – it takes the cake. It will probably go and get itself published somewhere just to haunt her for eternity. She'll go to fancy psych conventions and be the therapist with the horrible thesis.

But at least this thesis means something to her.

She slides the pages under the door and goes to the computer lab to click around apartments again while she waits for Trisha and Alex so they can have their traditional celebratory cocktails and greasy apps at the bar on Pike.

That's when she sees it.

She calls the owner and texts Oliver to meet her there. She tells Alex and Trisha that she'll meet them at the bar later and heads towards the address posted.

Just from outside, she knows this is exactly what she wants. Right now it has a sign outside that says Ye Olde Boston Bed and Breakfast. She can see why it's for sale, something like that wouldn't be popular in the city. She speaks with Jodi and Mike, the owners who are looking to relocate back into the county, their idea to bring a little kitch to the city not taking off as quickly as they'd planned.

The brownstone itself is beautiful. Right on the corner with a round tower jutting out of it, curved windows bringing in a lot of natural light into the odd shaped room that would be perfect for Oliver's studio. The downstairs is spacious, the kitchen closed off in its own little space with a dining room large enough for company. When you first walk in there's a hallway type room they have been using for check-ins that leads to double doors and a large living room beyond it.

To get upstairs you have to pass by the tower and through a doorway. Upstairs are two bedrooms about the same size, a bathroom and another small living room area.

It's beautiful and so perfect for where their lives are going. Upstairs could be their space and downstairs their work space, perfect for a small therapist's office for when she is licensed and lines up a few of her own clients.

But it has to be out of her price range. And if the owners are moving away, it probably isn't up for the rent she's hoping for. She can see Oliver passing outside and excuses herself to wave him in.

"What's wrong?" Is Oliver's first question.

"What?"

"You tell me to get to this address, no explanation, you donnae answer your phone—"

"Sorry, I turned it off. I was trying not to be rude. Just, come here, I want to show you something."

Oliver looks up at the Bed and Breakfast sign and waggles his brows back at her. "Oh. Your etchings?"

"Oh my God I'm going to pretend that I don't even know what that means. Oliver, this is Mike and Jodi, they're selling and we're looking to buy. Caught up?"

Oliver nods quickly, looking a little embarrassed at the possibility of people having overheard him before he does a double take of their surroundings. "Erm, Jae. This place is…"

"Spacious?" Jodi pitches in, nodding quickly herself. She is very excited at having buyers. Apparently dealing with realtors hadn't gone well.

"Yes. Indeed. Maybe more spacious than we can afford though?" He looks back at Jaeli who is thinking the same thing.

"We haven't gotten around to a price tag yet actually…" She says turning back to Jodi. Craigslist had said one dollar, she's positive that isn't true.

"Ah." Oliver says giving Jaeli the side eye. "Well, can we have a look around and maybe think about that price tag?" Oliver asks. Sam leads the tour again, Oliver picking up little things that might be a problem in the future that Jaeli had been too taken aback to see. She is a little smug that there isn't much wrong. She has enough sense to notice if the roof is going to fall on her head, thank you. It's just little things like asking about what kind of heat they have and checking to see if the water ran. Jaeli probably would have been too polite to do something like that even if she did think of it anyway. Who does that? Men apparently.

When it finally does come down to the price, the website had been right, they were looking to rent. Jaeli takes a deep breath at that. She would have felt awful for springing this on Oliver if she had been *that* wrong.

It's a little out of her price range, but she has to think of everything. If they got an apartment that was unfurnished that meant, appliances. Those weren't cheap. Mike and Jodi were leaving the fridge and oven and said they could work on it being utilities included. They offer some of the furniture at a low price too which Jaeli says they would think about. Just because she got an apartment she could turn into a private practice in the future didn't mean she needs office furnishings right now.

They talk it out back and forth for a while, Jaeli getting tired and just wanting to go home and think, but Jodi has a hungry look in her eye like she's played this game before and if they went home she knew they weren't coming back.

Mike and Jodi leave them in one of the upstairs bedrooms to think for a bit, *blocking the exits* she thinks to herself. Jaeli looks to Oliver who is looking at her with an indecent amount of pity.

"What did you get yourself into Jae?"

"It didn't look anywhere near this big online and it was posted as a dollar per month. I knew that was wrong but I had to call and see what it really was and then... I didn't really think it would be so high until I saw the sign, but they were waiting and it was too late. It's beautiful though isn't it? And there's room for a studio for you and an office for me." She breaks off with a sigh.

"They still haven't come down in price yet."

"But they're so eager. You don't think they'll work with us a little?"

"How about we set a price and if they can't meet it, we walk. It's not that hard Jae."

Jaeli set her chin and nods. "Okay. What do you think?"

"What are you paying now?"

CAUGHT IN A LIE

"800, but it's got a campus discount. I think they're 1200 normally."

"For tha shite hole, yeah we can't afford this." Oliver crams his hands in his hair.

"Oliver. Come on. Help."

"I'm helping, I'm helping. Alright, how much higher can you afford to go?"

"Right now? Not much. The second I pick up my diploma I'm going to start getting bills for my loans. I might be able to do 1200, but if I can't find a job right away, we're not going to be here long."

"I can chip in. I make about 325 a month at the café and I could get Rose to send me a little again. So like, 2000?"

"Rose would give you that much?"

"She's collecting a paycheck for me. And I've been getting a lot of commissions through the website."

"You really like this place too, don't you?"

"I really like how excited you are."

"Alright. So less than 2000 or we walk."

"Right."

Mike and Jodi are looking for thirty one hundred, they don't walk.

They do however, negotiate to not move in or start paying rent, just to be clear, until the end of August when Jaeli's lease would run out and she'll almost have her license.

They're going to come back to sign papers the next Monday.

CHAPTER SEVENTEEN

Jaeli gives the good news to her mother that weekend before their meditation. It prompts a very happy session complete with a special dinner afterwards where they share the news with her sisters. She shows them the pictures she took on her phone after touring through one last time so she could 'plan décor' she told Jodi, she had really just wanted the pictures.

Her mother gives Jaeli her graduation present early, five hundred dollars in a glittery card. "I thought you could buy the nice working clothes but you pay the rent, okay." Her mother pats her hands around the money that Jaeli feels horrible for taking, especially with Marianna's eyes on them.

While she's in Rhode Island, she calls up her boss at CCSRI to talk about her supervised hours again and about the possibility of a job after she's licensed. It's not guaranteed, but she likes Jaeli's approach to therapy. She's told that should her hours go well, and since she already knows most of their clients, her dream approach would make a good blurb in their brochure, bring in 'a more *natural*

CAUGHT IN A LIE

clientele'. Jaeli isn't going to argue with good news. She thinks of the brownstone waiting for her and the perfect little parlor to set up her office in, how she will decorate it and who she'll see there. She of course wants her own practice, but only once she's built up her own clientele, keeping a couple days at CCSRI couldn't hurt. She wants that base, therapists to talk to and get opinions from, she doesn't want to be alone in her career. This past year has been good at showing her that.

When she gets home to Oliver Sunday night it's to a peck on the cheek, dinner on the counter and his own set of pictures set out with a list of things he wants to buy and were they would go. She's glad she hadn't bullied him into the move, that he is as excited about it as she is. Especially since she'll be starting hers CAGs classes soon and not spending as much time with him again.

"You think maybe we can bless it?" He asks, doodling a little outline of his future studio.

"Bless it?" Jaeli asks, she hasn't known Oliver to be religious. She looks up from her plate to see a particular brand of smirk on his face. "Oh! You mean Christen it." She laughs and winked his way. "It's a possibility."

"Tease." He shakes his head, going back to work.

Jaeli is on her last bite when her phone starts ringing back on the counter. She takes her plate over to the sink and picks it up to see Marianna's face frowning at Mud, a silly picture Ariel had taken Saturday night that Jaeli loves. "Hey Mars. What's up?"

"I think he's hoarding away money from me."

"Well hello to you too. And what are you talking about?"

"He's still smoking."

"Ok?"

"We can't afford that! And I know what he gets paid, we have direct deposit and I have control of the bills since the credit card disaster. He's not taking any money out that I can tell, but he's still getting cigarettes."

138

EMILY TALLMAN

"Well one, I think you should talk to Jason. This kind of mistrust is going to build, you're going to blow up at him and nothing good is going to come from that. Two, maybe he's just bumming from someone he works with?" Jaeli has a feeling that isn't the case, and from their interactions the past few weekends, she honestly wonders if they were really talking about cigarettes.

"No, because I've been thinking about it. He never brings home tips. I think he's squirreling them away or something. Why would he do that? Ariel doesn't even have any birthday presents bought yet and he's just smoking away the money? Why would he do that?"

"You should ask him."

"I think he's saving up for a lawyer. Or maybe a hotel or a car or something. He's going to leave us Jae. With nothing."

"You don't have nothing. You have options, you can sell the house instead of trying to rebuild. I know mom would welcome you back permanently with open arms—"

"That's not the point! You've got to help us."

"I'm trying to Mari."

"It'll be all your fault when he does something stupid." The line goes dead and she throws her own phone across the room. God help her if her patience with people is already disappearing. She isn't even a therapist yet. Maybe she does need the mandatory therapy she's been in.

"Everything okay love?"

"Just sisters."

"Aye. You should've grown up with mine."

Jaeli chuckles and moves back to her seat across from him at the table, laying her head down on her arms and watching him draw. "It was Mari."

"Tch, she is a tough one. How'd it go?"

CAUGHT IN A LIE

"My mom gave me five hundred dollars towards our first rent and she wants it. She didn't say it in as many words but… I mean she does deserve it more doesn't she?"

"Mm. Your mam is giving her a home right now and who knows what else. Don't feel bad love. If you want, give her the money, if you want to keep it, you've worked very hard and your mam would have given it to ya anyway. Right? For graduating and yer birthday?"

"Look at you being all wise."

"I heard you found it attractive."

"You think you're so cute."

"Wheesht. So do you."

"Unfortunately." Oliver gives her a quick smile and she goes on to confirm her position in her licensure class and pay for the book. Summer and one more semester. Then who knows, she could be rolling in clients and help Mari in the way she wants if not necessarily the way Jaeli thinks she needs.

Summer goes by with beach dates, a nice slow paced CAGs programs, her licensing on its way and over half of her supervised hours completed. They go to a production of Hamlet that Theo stage manages on his own and has a small roll in and on many nights out with their friends. If this is what her future looks like, Jaeli is looking forward to it.

The calls from home aren't as frequent as she expects after that first Marianna explosion. Mostly Ariel asking for what she called fun auntie days and Scott asking to crash at her apartment during a gaming convention she wonders how he can afford. They both get a drive by view of the brownstone and are very impressed.

Before they know it, the end of August is here, the lease is almost up and a moving van is being packed. Her landlord has a very energetic happy dance for the removal of the Pod, middle fingers included, and Jaeli takes one last look through their empty little home of the last couple years. She's going to miss it, but she is way too excited for the space of their new home to get too emotional.

When they move, her friends are too busy to help them out on a work day, but they manage well enough on their own. If everything isn't completely unpacked, it's at least in neatly labeled boxes and stacked neatly in the room it belongs to.

And Christened the studio certainly is. And the bedrooms, bathroom and kitchen. They'll get everywhere eventually.

The next weekend is the first weekend in a while where she doesn't want to get in the car and take the long drive to visit her mother. But they have a deal, and she does want to check on Marianna. Still, she has a bad feeling that won't quit the entire time she's gone. She checks in with Oliver who seems cheery enough and even texts Trisha, Alex and Theo but everything seems in order.

It doesn't stop her horrible dreams about the hooded stranger. Dreams that have intensified in their violence since her first date with Oliver. Dreams where she's always too late to save him.

She leaves earlier than usual Sunday, but she's honest with her mother who becomes worried as well, even if she tries to hide it, her mother expresses pride that Jaeli is finally listening to her senses.

Darkness is always a big part of her dreams. Too dark to see the broken window, too dark to see the stranger lurking. Jaeli thinks the bright September sun will serve as protection, will mean she is right on time and everything will be perfectly fine. She lets the sun shine on her as she picks up Thai food down the block from home and takes her time finding a parking space and walking up the block and around the corner.

She should have known better.

Chapter Eighteen

Jaeli has the time to ask herself after the fact why she lied so much. Why was it so comfortable? How was it her go to as a conversation tool?

Is it for attention? Maybe, when she was younger. Maybe she wanted to be the pretty one, the fun one, the popular one that never sat alone at the crowded lunch tables, but got to talk to the person next to her. Maybe to be someone who had something to do during recess or who had people actually show up to her birthday parties.

Looking at herself now though, she didn't think that this was the answer. Everyone leaves. No one stays nice. Everyone eventually sees something in her that they don't like and that's when she ends up alone. Maybe she doesn't lie to bring people close. Maybe she lies to protect herself. To keep people at a distance. A little preemptive push away before they decide to leave on their own.

***

Jaeli is still nervous, but feeling much better when she gets home and bounces into the room that would be her office one day soon to see Oliver so close and whole and alive. She sets the food down on the window sill as all of the table like surfaces in that room are still covered in boxes.

"You think I should get some plants for the window? Jaeli asks, running a finger over the slightly dusty sill. There are little water mark circles worn into the old wood from over watered pots past.

"*I was never anything but honest with Olli.*" Oliver says in an odd tone. Jaeli freezes, Thai food and plants forgotten. She steps back towards him and notices that maybe he isn't as whole as she first thought. Her brows furrow as she tries to figure out what he's talking about, but then she rounds some boxes and sees what he's holding. He's sitting on the coffee table next to the box of paper work she has been organizing into shred and keep piles. There is an essay in his hands. He rolls it up and gestures at her with it, eyes angry and hurt like Jaeli has never seen. "Yeah, Jae. It sure feels like it."

"Olli." Is all she can say, falling back on that magic fix-it nick name that has always made him smile at her. He isn't smiling this time.

"How can you even call me that? Doesn't the name taste dirty in your mouth after everything?" Jaeli looks back down at the paper in his hands and can't look away. It's been so long, over two years of panicking and wondering when it would happen and she has never really prepared for it. He knows. Oliver must see the recognition in her eyes because a finger shoots up, telling her to wait. "Hold on a minute. I'm still processing my horrible death."

"It… I mean, it wasn't you. Not really."

"Cleary. Christ Jaeli, why? I mean, so many frankly *weird* conversations with your friends make sense now."

CAUGHT IN A LIE

"I told you I had written a story. That first time we met, I told you—"

"Yeah. But you didn't tell your family it was just a story, did you? That your little friend Olli wasn't real. Do they think we've been dating all these years because Marianna's nowhere near as crazy as I thought if so. And then our friends..." Oliver stops and laughs out a harsh noise she doesn't care to hear again. "You didn't tell me it was supposed to be true and all of your friends thought it was. My God, do you realize how insane this is? Our friends think you went through this horrible, traumatic thing and that I'm reminding you of it every day and being completely insensitive about it. I didn't even know. Is any of this even true? Why would you lie like that? Or why would you not tell me something like this happened to you? Which one is it and what was his real name because I am sorry if you did go through this, but somehow I don't think it happened. "

Jaeli's world drops away. This is everything she didn't want. Everything she could feel slotting into place that first day in the bakery. He isn't her own personal miracle on 34th street, it's all some cruel joke from the universe and it is over now. What does she even say? The truth? Was telling the truth even worth it now?

"It was just a stupid creative writing class and we had to write about our most bitter sweet moment and everyone was so connected with their feelings, had these amazing stories and mine was supposed to be a happy one, but I just couldn't. It wasn't fair. And then, I just... and then at home..." Jaeli's face is burning. What is her excuse? Everyone was lying? She didn't want to tell any real stories? Why *did* she do this to herself? "I kept having these dreams so I just wrote them down instead. It wasn't ever supposed to be this big thing." She can't look at him, can't stand to see the disappointment and anger even though she deserves every bit of it.

"So you felt pressured into it by your classmates then? By your mam and your sister? That's your excuse?"

144

"No. I just wanted something for myself. Something that *I* was feeling and that I could bring to the table. A good story. A way to escape criticism and it just blew up!"

"Well, you had it, didn't ya. Something for yourself. You fucking had me. And you threw it away with these stupid lies. We have the same bloody name Jaeli! Am I that underwhelming that you had to spiff me up? Is tha really so bad Jae, that I'm following my dreams? That I'm supporting my art until it can support me? You're the one who told me that was okay. Was that a lie too? Hell, it's not like therapy is going tae make you a millionaire, or is that why you wanted one? Is that where you go on the weekends? Prowling for a better deal? Jesus, I thought you were different. Better."

"That's not—"

"You couldn't just say I was a twenty five year old college barista because I don't think that's so bad. Not knowing what you want at twenty five. But I'll sure as hell tell you what I don't want in my life right now. "

It feels like everything moves into slow motion as Oliver stands, slammed the pages down and leaves the room. She can hear him stomping and slamming around, glad he at least isn't storming out of the apartment all together before he comes back into view with an overflowing box. Tears slide down Jaeli's cheeks, her knees hit the floor, and all she can think about is the stupid, badly written scene where FakeOliver dies in the hospital. She is such an idiot.

"Oliver, please." She doesn't hear the door open or slam like she's been expecting so she decides to continue. Maybe if he'd just listen. "I wrote that before I even met you. It was never supposed to go this far, I swear. I'm an idiot and losing you is probably karma or something but don't you think it's just a little weird that my brain conjured up this image of you, name and everything when we weren't even in the same country? And then we actually meet and… isn't it just weird? How are we supposed to ignore that?

CAUGHT IN A LIE

Maybe…maybe it's some strange twist of fate. Or maybe I'm psychic like my mother thinks. That's where I go on the weekends Olli. To her. She's trying to get me to open up my senses, to trust them and I have been. I changed my thesis and my direction of study. Because of you. Just… let's figure it out okay?"

"Psychic?" Oliver scoffs under his breath, accent thick with anger, sounding not at all like the charming, happy creature he was when she had found him, but stripped bare and threatening, showing his teeth. "For a second there I actually t'ought you were starting tae be honest with me, but this is all just another story for you tae tell. Got any other superpowers there Jae? Hiding a cape and helmet in one of these boxes?"

"Oliver—"

"We're done here."

"Olli I'm telling the truth!"

"*And I don't believe you.*" He yells back. This time the door does open and Jaeli feels the slam in her bones.

CHAPTER NINETEEN

J aeli let's herself have the night. One night to cry and be angry and miserable and eat everything in sight and just feel horrible before she picks herself up in the morning and calls her therapist.

Her last session had been the month before finals, but she says it's an emergency and is given an appointment same day.

She goes through her classes, ignoring Trisha and Alex's phone calls, a call from Catherine and one from her mother too.

When she finally lets herself plop down and curl into the under stuffed suede chair in Sadie's office she lets herself gather her thoughts and take a deep breath before coming clean.

"Do you ever feel like you can't breathe? Like maybe you've been looking at *everything* wrong and there is just no possible way to get yourself out of the hole you've dug?"

Her therapist waits, hands folded in her lap and not quite making eye contact with Jaeli, waiting for her to continue. Jaeli doesn't, she has asked a question, she wants an answer. "I think we all feel that way sometimes, but we can always talk about it with someone. You know that. And most times the other person's words will build ladders for you to climb out of that hole and try again."

Jaeli wondered if she will be able to spout little metaphors like that when she's practicing someday.

"I can tell what you're thinking Jaeli, and let me tell you, the best clinicians seek out therapy of their own. Everyone needs help from time to time. That's why I'm here. I rely on my peers for support and advice just like anyone else in any other job. So why don't you tell me what's bothering you and we'll see if I can do something about it."

"Everything. I ruined absolutely everything with that stupid paper." Jaeli says dramatically, she knows. She bites her lips hard and tries to steady her breath and not cry. It is bad enough that she opted to lay down today instead of sit like a regular, respective, modern day patient and not one of Freud's girls. Sadie lets the silence linger, not wanting to stop the flow of words Jaeli has let out with her any of own, but knowing when to prompt instead of pressure.

"We're not talking about the one from around the time we met, are we?"

"Yes! God, it's never going to go away. I thought I could just ignore it but it's just, uh!" Jaeli sighs, she tries to tamp down her emotions again. "I never told my friends it wasn't real. And then I did worse. I let my family think that the guy I wrote about was real to get them off my back and now, now he is real! He is an actual person, he knows my friends, my family. We were going to move in together and then he found the goddamn paper and thinks I'm this horrible person, which I probably am, and he's going to tell everyone and you know, for the first time in my life it felt like I had something. Like I trusted someone with everything. Like maybe he'd still be there five years from now, ten and we'd be good for each other. And my friends, I thought they were the best friends forever type, but he's going to tell them, if he hasn't already, I know it and you were right. I ruined everything and it's too late to fix. I'm the worst."

Jaeli is prepared for the *I told you so's*. She knows it wouldn't be ethical, but it's what she thinks will come her way none the less. She isn't prepared for calm and patient advice. She knows she's tuning most of it out, but the communication part sticks. So did the give him space. She thinks she knows how to do both and gives it her best shot when she gets home.

She pulls up the tumblr they have been working on together, sees the ask box alight with questions and submissions, but ignores it for making a text post.

Jaeli puts up a note that the artist is going through a hard time emotionally and won't be posting for a while. She lets Oliver's followers know that questions and comments aren't being ignored, he just needs some space. She let them know that she's sure his next piece will be all the better for it because she believes in him.

It might be a little passive aggressive, but how else is she supposed to talk to him while giving him room to think. The least she can do is show him she's still here, right?

She checks the website everyday just in case, but nothing s posted until Friday.

Friday morning she goes to the site and sees a painting he posts of their living room with one of his cloaked figures clutching a bunch of papers in its hands. She recognizes her one leg wrapped in the red patterned skinny jeans she was wearing in the foreground, an end of her scarf just visible.

She's made one of his paintings and it feels horrible.

Chapter Twenty

Jaeli has been avoiding the downstairs as much as possible. Bad memories have been her excuse. But it has officially been six days, Oliver's things are still everywhere and she doesn't know what to do with herself upstairs anymore. She thinks she can start unpacking the things in her office, maybe straighten out his boxes so he can come and get them when he's ready. She should probably just be packing everything, because she's not going to be making rent on her own for long.

She has been responding to her friend's texts on and off, even if she's still avoiding seeing them in person, it's nice to know they are somewhat there. She finds out through Trisha that Oliver is squatting in their old apartment. Theo has tried to get him to move in with him and Alex, but he's avoiding them too. She doesn't seem to know the reason, just that Oliver was trying to surprise Jaeli with unpacking everything and that he stumbled upon a secret that upset him.

EMILY TALLMAN

She knows she trusts him, but she really thought he would have taken it upon himself to tell them by now. She feels so guilty that she has to stop texting for a while, focusing back on the job at hand.

Jaeli is going through the cutesy office supplies Trish gave her as a graduation present, peeling open a package of multicolored, heart shaped post-its when all of a sudden the room is a little too dark. She pulls the chain on her desk lamp and then the lamp on an end table. Neither work. She pockets the post-its and goes on a quest for light bulbs as the sun sets further. When she has torn through every Wal-Mart and grocery bag in the place with a surprising lack of light bulbs she finally admits to herself that she forgot to buy them. Apparently the only working light is in her bedroom. She wishes she were a little more surprised, but it's not like she's left her room enough to notice the last few days. She lets out a heavy sigh, one straight from the soul as she rounds back to the kitchen and sees the message pad on the fridge proudly proclaiming in Oliver's neat scrawl *light bulbs*. She pulls out her phone and debates over three names before just going with her gut. "Hey Marianna."

"Hey. You didn't come down this weekend. Mom was getting worried." She thinks she heard Jason say something in the background but carries on anyway. Best to get it all out before she caves.

"Um, anyway …can I come tonight and maybe stay with you guys for a few days? Maybe a week?"

There's a pause from the other end of the line before it sounds like the television is turned down further and her sister is shushing someone. "What's wrong with your nice, new place?"

Jaeli looks around the dark room she had such high hopes for. It all just feels wrong now. "Well, it's kind of empty and it's creeping me out. I haven't even finished unpacking yet and I think I forgot to buy light bulbs and it's getting dark. I just thought, maybe a couple days home—" would be a nice distraction, she thinks as her sister cuts her off.

CAUGHT IN A LIE

"What about Oliver?" Ugh, maybe not. But she has to admit the truth sometime.

"We kind of split." That is an understatement. She isn't expecting the fury that blasts down the line strong enough to make her jump back.

"Is he kicking you out? Jaeli! I will kick his ass to the curb so fast-"

"NO. No, he left. He's back at my old place. It's nothing. I'm just. I don't know Mars, I'm lonely and I just don't feel right." Her stomach has been churning and her heart is pounding from more than the angry shout and surprise. She's anxious about something, it has been niggling the back of her mind all day and now that she knows what the feeling is, she almost wants to throw up.

"So he's home?" Jaeli rolls her eyes, how was she supposed to know? She sits back next to the boxes marked 'office' and digs the post-its out of her pocket, picking at the plastic wrapping.

"Yeah, I guess. Why are you so hung up on Oliver? For once *I* kind of need *you*. And don't do anything stupid Mars, it's my fault." She feels a little guilty at the attitude she's giving off when asking for a favor, but seriously, how often has she given her sister a shoulder to cry on? Could she not just spend one night with her? Jaeli hears her move the phone to her chest and say something. She sighs into the phone, seriously?

"Sorry. No, I'm not. I just, I don't know. Jason is really late."

"What does that have to do with anything?"

"Aren't you the one that says we need to make more decisions together? I don't know. I just wanted to ask him if it was okay, that's all. I guess you can come over. I'll tell mom. Or maybe Ariel can stay over at your new place. She can go pick up light bulbs with you. She always has fun with you, maybe she can help unpack and cheer you up."

"I guess." Normally Jaeli would jump at the chance to spend time with her niece, corrupt her with some fun TV channels Mari

152

EMILY TALLMAN

blocks and too much ice cream, but the pain in her gut is spreading and her heart is feeling jittery. She doesn't think she'd be much of a fun auntie tonight.

"So what happened? Tell your big sister." What to say? She could go with the 'I don't want to talk about it', but then that wasn't a great case for asking to stay over. What was she going to do at home anyway? Park herself on the couch and ignore her sister's questions?

"We had a fight. A big one. He was going through some stuff I had written and I don't know. It really upset him. I tried to tell him that the story was nothing, it wasn't really about him, but he wouldn't listen and he just left. Loudly and angrily. Said I was lying, I don't know." Jaeli sniffles back some tears. It isn't the first time she has cried since he slammed the door. Maybe she just needs the release.

"So how is that your fault? Unless you *were* lying?"

Jaeli laughs through the tears, how does she even start to explain that disaster? She puts the phone on speaker and moves it to the coffee table in front of her as she wipes away a few fat tears and goes to town on the overprotective plastic wrap. The plastic finally snaps and the little stack of hearts fall out onto the floor. The colorful mess sparks something in her. A memory almost. She looks back to the phone and sees the date. It's Oliver's birthday. "Hey?" She hears herself ask. "Hey, is Jason home yet?"

It takes a nerve wracking minute for Marianna to answer with a bored tone. "No, not yet."

"I just have this really bad feeling. I think I've got to go"

"Wait! What about Ariel?" The phone asks as she picks up the paper hearts and grabs a sharpie.

"Tell her maybe next weekend. I've got to go." She grabs her keys and flies out the door. She needs to see Olli. Maybe she has this whole thing backwards. Jaeli hopes she still has time to fix it.

Chapter Twenty One

The dusk turns to full night as she writes out an apology on the sticky hearts, sitting in her car in her old parking space. Jaeli is wasting time, she knows this. Full on chickening out. She could be doing this right at the door, knocking when she's done and running away then. It would give her more of a chance of seeing Oliver, but she tells herself that would be creepy and this way is better.

When's she finally ready to climb the stairs up the center of the building to her old place, she hears a bang and freezes. She's heard that same sound a million times before. She backs up to the railing and sees the sliding glass window four floors up broken with a piece of the curtain wafting through the hole. She bolts up the stairs, dialing 911 as she goes, distractedly shouting that there's a break in and the address as she reaches the door and shoves her way in, right into two men fighting over the gun she had heard go off. Oliver looks over at her in a panic as she shoves the hooded man to the side.

Something in her recognizes the coat this time, knows it's Jason and she has a moment to think that this is all her fault before there's pain exploding in her ribs and her ears are ringing as another shot is fired. The force of it slams her into the wall, the back of her head exploding in pain. If she had never said anything, never let her family think this Oliver was the rich idiot from her stories, maybe Jason would have never gotten it in his head to do something so dangerous and stupid. She curls into herself, reaching down and expecting her hand to find warm wetness, but only causing herself more pain.

Oliver takes over Jason in an instant, giving him a solid punch to his shocked face that he couldn't get the leverage for before. And then he's over her, gently easing Jaeli onto her back and trying to move her hand away. He looks confused for a moment, lifting Jaeli's shirt when the police swarm in.

She has a few seconds to think about how fast that was before everything goes dark.

CHAPTER TWENTY TWO

When Jaeli comes to it's in a very bright room with a nurse waving a light in her eyes, another off to the side with Oliver.

She can't help turning to him, but the sensation of her brain backstroking in her scull has her instantly regretting it. "Are you okay?" She mumbles out. Her tongue is sticking to her mouth in that specific way that means she is on some serious pain killers. She's pretty okay with that, last thing she remembers was some serious pain, so you know, at least she's alive.

"Am I..?" Oliver asks throwing up his hands and storming out of the room.

Jaeli looks to the nurse before trying her best to fight her way out of the blankets. "No, no. Absolutely not. You have a head injury. I'm sure he'll come back, he's been very worried."

Worried is good right? Better than indifferent. He could have just left her in the empty apartment to bleed out and taken their lovely brownstone for himself. Worried meant he still felt things, right?

She finishes her checkup and is scolded for scratching the back of her head before she figures out the sensation is staples and immediately grabs the far too small sick bowl to throw up. She's so glad she wasn't awake for that. Just remembering how it had looked when Oliver needed staples nearly has her hurling again and the pain in her ribs and stomach really isn't ready for that. Oh God, she probably has stitches there too. How long has she been out?

When she's settled again, the nurses leave and Oliver comes back to stand in the doorway a few minutes later. She takes him in, just soaking up the image of him afraid to speak in case she scares him away.

"I called your ma."

"Thanks." She whispers. They're silent again and a pain is flaring in her that she doesn't think any grade of drugs is going to numb. "Will you sit? Just for a sec?"

Oliver clears his throat and continues to hover before he breaks, stumbling over to the chair by her bed and sitting heavily into it.

"What happened?"

"Your arsehole of a brother in law tried to rob us. Me I guess. I dinnea ken. Did you know he was going to do that?"

"No!" Jaeli yells. She wasn't surprised when it happened, that bad feeling inside her boiling over and knowing it was Jason as soon as she got through the door but she didn't know her dream was actually going to come true and not like this. "I swear Olli. Oliver. I talked to Marianna and it gave me a weird feeling and then I just needed to talk to you. To make things better somehow. I was going to leave a message on the door, but I saw the glass and… I don't know. I just had to make sure you were okay. Are you?"

"I'm fine Jae. I saw it too. I remembered reading it and it just seemed weird. I thought it was a prank but called the police just in case and when I got there he was going crazy that the apartment was empty. I just wanted him to put down the gun and then you got there. Why did you do that? Jump a man with a gun? Are you crazy?"

Jaeli bites her shaking lip and breaths deep against the numb pulse beating in her head. "I was always too late. In the dream. And I spent so much time on the stupid note and I thought it was going to happen again and I just couldn't. I couldn't watch you die."

"Jaeli. That wasn't me. I'm not what you want."

"Yes you are. The dream, the nightmare whatever, it was all about things leading up to the robbery, whether you want to believe that or not. The pieces about him being rich and the flowers and that garbage, it was stories from where Catherine works. It was filler. Three AM paper deadline, word count filler."

Oliver laughs a bitter thing Jaeli doesn't care to hear coming from him and shakes off the conversation. "I don't want to talk about that. Alright. Just don't or I won't wait for your family to get here, I'll just leave Jae I swear."

Jaeli lets herself cry. She's done being strong, if that's what she has even been all this time. She nods.

"Fine. So, Jason got arrested. I haven't decided if I'm pressing charges or not but at the time, he shot you Jae. I didn't know the gun wasn't real and you were out cold so I let them take him."

"Wasn't real?" Jaeli asks wetly, it sure as hell felt real.

"It was just BBs. Your head was worse. You hit it on the door going down." Oliver laughs a bit brighter though he's swabbing at his eyes a bit too roughly. "You did about as well with the robbery as I did with the mugging. Head wound worse than your gun shot. Still a nice bruise though and a little nick of blood. You might even get a scar." Oliver wipes a hand down his face, bracing his elbows and letting his hands almost touch the bed.

The silence stretches on until Jaeli can bring herself to talk again. "You know the part with the broken window? I added it in later. The professor, he told me I needed foreshadowing and I told

EMILY TALLMAN

him real life doesn't have foreshadowing. That's how this whole thing started. Trisha and Alex were in that class and the next where I was handing in the paper again because I ran out of time to write two. So if I told them it wasn't real, I could have gotten in serious trouble academically. At the time school was the most important thing to me. I didn't know you guys yet." Oliver stays silent, staring off into space. He doesn't look like he's going to leave yet so she keeps going. "The professor, he told me to go back and add in what I wish I had noticed the first time, maybe something that could have prevented it, something that could have changed the outcome. So I put in the broken window and the curtain. I don't even remember if that was in the original dream." She sniffles and closed her eyes against the cold silence.

"If you ever see him again, remember to thank him for that bit of constructive criticism for me. Okay?"

She hums a little laugh at him that she wouldn't be capable of without the drugs and lets herself slip into sleep again.

She has a horrible, confusing dream about Oliver with that look on his face from the Sunday he found out mixed up with him lying in the hospital bed and is glad to escape it when a hand nudges her awake.

She's so glad to see Oliver that she can't help but spurt the first thing that comes to her. "Hi. My name is Jaeli Tal and can I say that you have amazing eyes." It's not colorful hearts or dozens of flowers, but it's theirs and maybe that's what she should have aimed for from the start.

"Well, using my own first words against me eh?" Oliver pushes himself out of the creaky hospital chair and looks like he's about to leave. She panics. "You're mam should be here before you need to be woken up again." It's now or never.

"No it's not that. The first time I saw them in real life they were so dark but beautiful I got lost for a bit. Kind of like when I look at your paintings. But then I saw them in the sunlight and these

CAUGHT IN A LIE

bright blue flecks were glowing at me and I knew I was in trouble. I dream about those eyes a lot Olli. Dreams aren't supposed to come true. So, please let me say I'm sorry for not reacting properly and let me start over."

Oliver doesn't look at her, just pauses on his way out, like he had that day, willing to give her one more chance, to be honest, to convince him. She has to be able to do it this time.

"Hi, my name is Jaeli Tal and when I was in school I would get bored while taking notes and think about your freckles. I found myself thinking of how fun it would be to play connect the dots with them. I even have notebooks to prove it." She stops for a breath and to smile to herself, hiding from the eyes peeking over at her. "By my calculation you have one hundred and forty one on your face alone, but I'd love the chance to double check."

Oliver doesn't answer but he's openly looking at her now, body facing her instead of the door and everything.

"Hi, my name is Jaeli Tal and your laugh is the most beautiful thing I've ever seen or heard. Every time I see you laugh, it makes me wish I could come up with more way to make you laugh."

Oliver clears his throat again, looking right into her eyes for a breathtaking few seconds before holing out his hand to her. "Hi. Mi name's Oliver Scott. I was supposed to be a Ross, like mi mams family name, but mi sister had to go an be born a Rose and my mam isn't kitch enough to have kids with matching names like that."

"It's a pleasure to meet you Oliver Scott."

"Mmm." Oliver hums. "Just you wait."

Jaeli still hasn't stopped laughing when her frantic family rushes into the room. How could she when she was this happy and Olli was doing that full body laugh right along with her? He finally shuts her up with a kiss, just as perfect as their second one.

"God I missed you. I underestimated how much I loved you when I said all tha *'you can't be in my life'* garbage."

"I really hope I'm not dreaming right now."

"I'll still be here when you wake up if you are. Just tell me that bit about my freckles again, okay?" He winks at her, only the flaring pain in her ribs keeping her from another giggle fit.

EPILOGUE

J aeli is let go as soon as her mother signs the paperwork that she will be looked after through the night and is given instructions about pain medication and how often to wake her up.

Her mother, Catherine and Mary end up staying for a few days. Oliver too, who officially moves back in. Marianna does make an appearance to apologize but doesn't stay long, whether out of guilt or anger Jaeli isn't sure yet. She has to believe it will work out.

Soon enough she's back to her work and school schedule, setting aside time to talk to Alex, Trisha and Theo who are all very upset but can't stay mad for long in the face of their worry. Jaeli can't help but sarcastically think that her timing in all of this has been kind of perfect. Oliver gives her a look that says he knows exactly what she's thinking.

At least she's getting a second chance, she can't ask for more. She can only hope for dreams of them all sitting outside their retirement home, wrinkled and reminiscing about the follies of their youth. It was the goal before, it can still be the goal now that they know the truth. Maybe someday it would even make Olli laugh.

When she does eventually open her own practice, Oliver paints the sign and helps decorate the office which has stayed unfurnished for too long. It was nice to use it as a show room for the auction Olli had hosted the December before, but it's time for a proper desk, filing cabinets and bookcases. She needs a couch, one with the appropriate amount of stuffing and the perfect coffee table. Jaeli is a little excited and maybe going a little overboard.

Especially when Oliver finds her contemplating the price tag on a table with a glass top you could see through to the moss growing underneath. Or maybe it was dried. She has been dreaming of moss a lot lately, growing up trees, clinging and thriving in a lonely, dark rain. Maybe she should get moss pots for the window sill instead of the flowers she's been debating. "What do you think about moss for the window?

"Moss, Jae. Really? When you said plants I was thinking like a fern or a cactus. Something that would forgive you if you forget to water it." He knows her so well.

"Moss is stronger than it looks. And I'm not sure. It feels important. Maybe we could make one of those little succulent gardens or a piece of live art."

Oliver sighs. "You're a strange one Ms. Tal. Good thing you're cute."

About the Author

This Rhode Island native has wanted to be a storyteller since hearing her first bedtime fairytale. She asked for a word processor for Christmas at age four and has kept her promise to Santa by writing every day since.

Her first series of books has been set in motion with the hope of making mental illness a more readily accessible topic. She writes characters with mental illness as the heroes with the goal that more people will see themselves as worthwhile individuals and no longer just horror movie villains. *Caught in a Lie* is the second book in the series which began with *Life in the Shadows*.

Emily's love of the supernatural, science fiction, and fantasy will surely be explored in later works of fiction, romance, and children's books.

Stay tuned at *www.emilytallman.com*

Made in the USA
Lexington, KY
10 November 2019